RUN AWAY
LEE

Larry L. Eddings

ISBN-13:978-1481070911
ISBN-10:1481070916

DEDICATION

This book is dedicated to all runaways:
Those who run away
from school,
from home,
from relationships,
from themselves,
Only to find that for which they are looking
is often at the very place from which they ran.

ACKNOWLEDGMENTS

A special word of acknowledgement to all those who have discovered
what it's like to cease running and find out that life is a gift that can be
shared with those from whom they no longer have to run.

Some of these returned runaways have been an inspiration to me:
Colleagues who have decided to not "throw in the towel." and run.
Friends who did not run away from unveiled threats.
Parents who did not run away from their parental responsibilities.
My family who never runs away from anything.

PROLOGUE

The story that is contained in the following pages is purely fictional – except, of course, for the parts that are true.

The names of the people have not been changed to protect the innocent. These are names that many people have and to find non-existent names would be quite impossible. And besides, regardless of their name, no one is completely innocent.

CHAPTER 1

"Nooooooo! Watch out! It's coming right at us," I yelled as the truck slammed into the driver's side of our old pickup. I yanked my left arm up to cover my face. Glass shattered, horns honked, metal ripped and crumpled like so much aluminum foil. Then, everything went black!

I bolted upright in bed, awakened yet again from the relentless nightmare by my own screaming. Perspiration covered my forehead. My body shook. My heart raced. I sat up, put my elbows on my knees and cradled my face in my hands. I reached to pull the covers more tightly around me as I felt the now very familiar chill run down my spine.

"Lee Edwards," I cried out to myself, "get hold of yourself, man! It's not real. It's just a dream."

No, it isn't just a dream! It's a nightmare! And it's always the same. It's happened over and over again for what seems like an eternity.

Two of us are traveling down a road in a pickup. I never recognize the road or the pickup or the driver. It's always dark. I am always the passenger and it always seems like I am yelling something at the driver, but I can't remember what I'm trying to say to him. The driver is always a man, but I can never see his face to recognize him.

Then another rig, always with its lights off, runs a stop sign and crashes into the driver's side of our pickup. My reflex is always the same as I sit in the passenger seat. I yell "Noooooo! Watch out! It's coming right at us!" I put my left arm up to protect my face. And my yell wakes me up! Every time!

Always before, I was aware that, following the crash, the driver, whoever he was, was slumped over the steering wheel, with blood oozing from his nose and mouth. He appeared to be dead. I never knew for sure because my yelling woke me up in a cold sweat.

Tonight, for the first time in this recurring nightmare, I recognized the driver. My dad. The shock of recognizing him caused me to gasp for breath. I was awakened this time, not by my screaming, but struggling to breathe. It had been twenty five years since I had seen or talked with my dad. Now he shows up in my nightmare, dead.

I had heard somewhere that dreams, no matter how long it may seem, last for only a few seconds. Then, usually, after you wake up, you don't remember it anymore. Supposedly the brain is simply cleaning out old cells or thoughts that have no meaning anymore.

I don't know if that is true, but I do know that I couldn't get this nightmare out of my mind. It was as real as though I were wide awake when it happened. It persisted night after night for what seemed like months. No matter how much I tried to ignore it, nothing worked.

There were times when I found myself screaming at the top of my voice, "Leave me alone. Get out of my life!" It wouldn't quit, no matter how much I yelled. It would cease for a few nights but return with a vengeance.

I didn't have anyone with whom to discuss the nightmare. If only I had someone with whom to talk about it, there might be some intelligent release from the haunting and gnawing feeling deep in my insides that it was far more than just a dream. It was more like something from within my inner most self yelling at me that it was time.

Time for what? I wrestled with that question over and over. I finally decided that maybe it was time to tie together some loose ends of my life that had been dangling and creating unresolved issues in my profession and, more importantly, within myself. I couldn't figure out any other reason for its relentless invasion of my sleep and my life.

Finally I just gave up. I knew I had to do something about it. When the nightmare invaded my sleep once again with the recognition of my dad as the driver in the pickup, I knew something had to be done. After catching my breath and feeling my heartbeat settle, I found myself saying, *"Okay! Okay! I give up. I'll do it. Whatever it takes, I'll do it."*

I had to make arrangements to do what I knew needed to be done and yet it was last thing on earth I wanted to do. I had to go back to the town of Pryor, the place of my birth. I had little or no understanding as for what purpose. I had only that recurring nightmare and a driving sense of urgency that is what I must do.

Since my dad ultimately surfaced in the nightmare, it all seemed to be tied to my past, the place, my family and perhaps others from whom I had run away twenty five years ago. I had intentionally run away and I had intentionally planned to never go back. Twenty five years is a long time! Things cannot possibly be the same as when I left. I'm not the same as when I left.

CHAPTER 2

When I first left from home at the age of eighteen I did a lot of wandering. After all, I was a high school graduate. I was old enough to be out on my own. I wanted to see other parts of the world. I felt I had been cooped up in that little town long enough. Others may enjoy the small town and everyone knowing everyone else's business, but it wasn't for me. I had no idea where I was going or how to get there, but get away, I must.

It didn't take long to discover that running away wasn't all that it was cracked up to be. I hadn't taken the time to consider what was involved in leaving behind the things that I had taken for granted, like a comfortable bed to sleep in every night, food on the table at least three times a day, clean clothes that had been washed for me, and a safe place inhabited by people who cared what happened to me. Regardless, I knew that I had to leave. I did.

There were times when I felt like I was going to starve. Days would pass without having anything substantial to eat. I scrounged food from the garbage cans behind restaurants and slept in the doorways of deserted buildings. My clothes began to smell putrid. I had times when I could find no safe place to rest for the night. There were other times when I even thought about returning home. That thought quickly passed.

At the time, I knew that I couldn't handle all the high school classmates that pointed fingers at me. Going back had never been an option for me. I felt I had to keep going, not knowing where. The thought kept running through my mind, "Go east, young men." It was the opposite of what I had read and heard in school history classes, "Go west, young man."

With time, I became a survivor, of sorts, as a runaway. Anyway, that's how I consider myself. I had to learn a lot of survival techniques in order to stay alive.

I learned how to panhandle in some of the larger town, in order to get a few bucks for food. I later discovered that churches along the way had food and clothing banks that were available to people in need. Some of them even had one or two free meals during the week for homeless people. I discovered that it was a lot easier to take advantage of their help than it was to panhandle. Others handed out bus passes and would help me buy a bus ticket to the next unknown town.

Some of the churches served really good meals and so I learned which ones to frequent on the nights they served to the homeless. One evening I was enjoying what, to me, was a seven course meal of hamburger patties, potatoes, vegetables and pie. The people who did the serving were very cordial and appeared glad to provide free meals for people like me. I was really glad to get the food and found it to be a lot like the meals we used to have back home.

The guy sitting next to me was stirring his fork around through the food on his plate and I overheard him mumble, "This is garbage."

There was only the two of us at the table and I was somewhat surprised to hear a homeless man say that about a free meal.

"Boy," I said, "I think it tastes pretty good. I haven't had much to eat lately,"

"I'm used to eating steak," he replied. "This is garbage."

"Steak? How on earth can you afford steak? You rich or something? I thought you're homeless."

"Who said anything about affording it. I can't afford it. I just go into the grocery store and lift it out of the meat counter, put it in my pants and walk out."

"You mean you steal steaks?

"Yeah, and a lot of other stuff. They never miss it. They got lots more where that comes from."

"Man, aren't you afraid that you're going to wind up in the pokey if you keep that up."

"Nah, I've been doing it for a long time and haven't got caught yet. Besides, it ain't none of your business what I do, so keep your nose out of it."

He pushed his chair back from the table, "I gotta get out of here."

I noticed that his plate was clean. He had finished off his hamburger patty, potatoes, vegetables and pie at the same time he was complaining about it and while he was bragging about his ability to steal steaks without getting caught.

I can't remember ever seeing him again at any of the meals served in the churches I frequented. I couldn't help but wonder if some store manager managed to catch him with a couple of steaks stashed in his pants. And too, it crossed my mind that after he had stolen the steaks how did he manage to cook them? I determined that with his attitude, he probably ate them raw.

``````

Hitchhiking became my basic mode of transportation - something that I had never done in my life. I didn't have to. We
``````

always had a pickup or car or truck around the farm. When I learned to drive I had access to one or all of them, so I had never even thought about needing to hitchhike.

I had seen people standing alongside the road on occasion with their thumbs up in the air, so I tried it. Most of the times people who stopped to pick me up were cordial and willing to take me to their next destination or drop me off where I wanted. However, it didn't take me long to learn about the real dangers of that mode of transportation.

On one occasion I managed to escape from one old, grandfatherly type individual who picked me up in his pickup truck. It had been a long day on the road out in the middle of nowhere. I was tired and my feet hurt all the way to my knees. It seemed like hundreds of cars had passed me up without even slowing down. I was beginning to think that I would be sleeping alongside the road that night.

Then, just about the time I was ready to find a place to bed down for the night, a pickup pulled off the road ahead of me. When he stopped, I walked up beside his truck hoping that he had stopped for me.

"Hey," he said, " ya' looking for a ride?"

"I sure am," I answered. "It's been a long, hot day."

"Get in," he said.

I got into the truck, settled into the seat and fastened my seat belt."

"Hey, thanks for stopping and giving me a ride."

"Glad to do it." he said. "How far are you planning to go, young fellow?"

"I'm just headed east with no particular place in mind, but I'll go as far as you are going."

"Okay," he said. "I'll take you as far as I'm going, which is about fifty miles down the road. That's the next town and it's where I live."

He acted like a friendly old man with a warm smile and kind eyes. We rode for several miles just talking about the weather, his work, family, where I was from and that I was going to no place in particular and just general chit chat. I found him fairly easy to talk to.

There were times when we rode along in silence. I began to enjoy those quiet times while just looking at the countryside in the fading sunlight. Once in awhile I would doze off.

Then, as I woke up, I began to notice something that made me feel uncomfortable.

I have been blessed with very good peripheral vision. Each time I opened my eyes, he seemed always to be looking at me with his eyes examining my whole body, but especially my waist. I began to feel like he was undressing me with his eyes rather than keeping them on the road. The increasing level of discomfort began to take effect on my nerves and I became very uneasy.

Then, in one of my half awake times, the conversation changed to something that caught me off guard. .He began to ask me questions that I thought were a little too personal to answer. So I just made a grunting sound and pretended to doze off again.

Then he asked the question that blew me away. "Since you're head to nowhere in particular would you like to stop off at my place and spend the night?"

"No, I don't think so. I need to be getting on down the road."

"It will be late by the time we get there and I have a good bed you could sleep in."

"It's tempting, but I think I'll just keep trying to get another ride. Thanks anyhow."

"I was thinking," he said, "that you might want stay for the night and you might like to engage in some recreational sex?" as he called it. At the same time he placed his right hand on my leg and began to rub it. "

I was totally surprised and shocked by his sudden vulgar suggestion and unsolicited physical touching. I felt like I was going to vomit, even at the very thought of what he was suggesting and trying to do.

"No,' I yelled at him By then I was wide awake. "I never have and I don't intend to get involved now, especially with your kind, so get your filthy hands off my leg." I hit his hand with my knuckles. He yanked it back and took hold of the steering wheel.

Nothing like that ever happened in our little town of Pryor when I was growing up. At least, if it did, I didn't know about it. I had difficulty believing what I was hearing and experiencing. The shocked look on my face when I stared at him must have surprised him also. After I hit him and told him to get his filthy hand off my leg, he tried to return to general chit chat conversation in a weak effort to put me at ease.

"Now sonny, don't get all upset. I just thought...."

"I don't care what you thought. Stop this damn truck and let me out, you miserable pervert.

He began to slow down and pull over to the side of the road. As soon as he slowed, I jumped out of his truck and took off running like a scared rabbit.

That encounter conditioned me to always be cautious when coming into contact with people who pick up hitchhikers - especially the overly friendly ones.

I slept out under a tree that night. I felt safer there.

\\\\\\\\\

There were times when I got into the larger cities that I tried to relate to people in my own age group, some of whom were runaways like me. Some were a little older, but several were much younger. I thought that maybe it would be a safer crowd. However, I discovered that it was also a whole new scene for me. I began to realize how sheltered I had been as I grew up in my small, hometown community of Pryor, never having been exposed to homeless lifestyles, except on my wanderings across country. It was a whole different world out here.

Some of the girls I met had been abused as they sought shelter in larger towns. I met some who had run away from foster homes in which they had been placed by the state. They had experienced physical and sexual abuse by foster parents. Others were forced into what amounted to child labor in factories that were owned by those who they thought the state had assigned to protect them.

On occasion I would join other young people who had gathered around a fire in the deserted yard of a closed factory. I met up with young men my age who were trapped in the drug scene. They were involved in breaking and entering into homes and businesses to steal items that they knew they could sell to support their drug habits.

There were those who tried to get me involved in what they were doing.

"Hey man,' you gotta try this. It'll blow your cotton-picking mind. Wow! I've never been so high and, wow, man, this is way out."

"No, thanks, man," I said. "You go ahead and blow your mind and get spaced out, but it's not for me. I like to know what I'm doing."

"What's with you, man? Too good to share a joint with a friend? Who are you, mister goody two shoes?"

"Yeah," I said, "I guess that's what I am, a mister goody two shoes." I found reason for putting some distance between that kid and me. I never did figure out what "goody two shoes" meant.

I did know that I had learned enough growing up that I wanted nothing to do with stuff that would ruin my brain and get me in trouble with the law. I had no difficulty resisting the offer of drugs. I had only to look at the emaciated faces, arms with needle holes in them and red eyes and runny noses, to remind me that I certainly didn't want to end up looking and acting like that.

I did meet and became friends with one fellow who was a few years older than me. I guessed him to be about twenty five. HIs name was Arnold. He had been living on the streets for a couple of years and seemed to know his way around. He was always bragging about being "street savvy." He was one who showed me how to find the churches and other organizations in that particular city that feed and clothe people who live on the streets. That's how we met.

We hung out together for awhile before I felt that I needed to keep on "going east." He never offered me drugs during the time I knew him. He did offer to give me a ride to the next town.

"Where are you heading?" he asked as we sat on a park bench in one of the unnamed, larger towns along the way.

"I'm just headed east," I said, "but I don't have any place particular in mind."

"I'm headed that way myself," he said. "Why don't I give you a ride to where you want to go? I have a car parked a couple of blocks down the street."

All my defense mechanism rose to the surface. Since memories of a previous ride experience flashed through my mind, I told him, "No, thanks. I don't know yet if that's where I want to go, and besides, I wasn't even aware that you had a car. You haven't said anything about having one."

"Well, I didn't before, but I do have one now," he said. "I just picked it up a couple of days ago. It's a beauty; a little blue Mazda Miata sports car. I inherited it, you might say. I'm planning to climb in it and head out of town. It's getting late and I need to be on my way. If you want to ride along you're welcome. It'll give you a place to get in out of the weather for awhile and you'll be farther on down the road."

I was tired of wandering the streets and searching for a warm and dry place to sleep, so I agreed to go with him.

We walked down the side street toward where he said his car was parked. When we got within about a block of the place, he stopped suddenly and quickly stepped into a nearby alley. I was surprised. So I stepped in beside him and asked, "What's happening, man?" Why did you jump into this dark alley all of a sudden?"

He acted awfully nervous as he looked back around the corner of the building and pointed down the street.

"I can't give you that ride I promised," he said.

"Why not?" I asked.

"Look down the street and you'll see. The police have surrounded my car. I can't take you anywhere."

Sure enough. I stepped back out on the sidewalk and looked down the street. There were three police cars parked by the car that he had previously described as his. Policemen were shining their flashlights into the car while others were writing down the license plate numbers. Some had their phones to their ears, no doubt reporting that they had found a stolen car.

I turned back toward the alley and said, "Man, you were wanting me to go riding with you in a stolen car? What's the matter with you? What got you into stealing cars?"

I was talking to the back of a blurred shadow as I saw him running toward the other end of the alley. I leaned against the cold brick wall and heaved a sigh of relief that I never had opportunity to take a ride in that little Mazda beauty of a stolen car.

I started to avoid the larger cities as much as possible, for that seemed to be the places where the runaways congregated into gangs, supposedly for protection and other gang-related activities, like sniffing coke and stealing cars.

\\\\\\\

I was finally able to work my way across country doing odd jobs and avoiding places where I thought I might get into trouble with the local authorities. After what seemed like an eternity, I finally wound up in a small town on the coast of Maine. I hung around the village, doing any kind of work I could find to earn money for food and a place to sleep.

One day, while I was hanging around the local marina, a rugged looking, seaman type guy approached me to see if I was looking for work. I said "yes" without even asking what kind of work. I just needed to earn some real money. I was tired of washing dishes in an all night sleazy dump called a cafe. It should have lost its food license years ago.

"Have you ever done any fishing?" he asked.

"Yeah," I said. "I used to fish in a lake that we had on our farm back in the mid-west."

"Well, this is a lot different than fishing in a lake. This is ocean fishing."

"I've never done any ocean fishing," I said, "but I'm willing to give it a try, if you can use me." Little did I know!

For some reason he hired me on the spot to work on his lobster fishing trawler. I told him that I had never worked on a boat, or even been close to the ocean before I wandered into this little seacoast town.

My life had been lived out in the Midwestern plains country where people could be heard to say "You can see all the way to Kansas from here." I was a flatlander, raised on a farm where we grew corn.

However, I imagined that there was a certain sense of adventure tied to riding on the waves of the sea and smelling the salt air. Most of my early years involved listening to such adventure stories told by my parents and grandparents in the confined and safe atmosphere of the library of our farmhouse. I was excited about this new adventure about which I had read, but in which I had never had the opportunity to participate. Now I could actually go to sea and experience it firsthand.

That excitement and fairy tale sense of adventure didn't last long once I got personally involved with an actual ocean.

The work on the lobster trawler was hard. The work was not a problem as I had learned to work hard on the farm. The working of the lobster traps and the lifting of the assorted weights, ropes and pots, served to build up my young adult muscles and create within me a sense of grown-up independence.

However, being out on the ocean beyond the sight of land was a new thing for me. All I knew before was "fields of waving grain," as the song says, but out here it was water as far as the eye could see with wave upon wave upon wave rolling one upon the other upon the other.

I think that is what finally got to me – wave upon wave upon wave, rolling one upon the other upon the other upon the other. It wasn't too bad as long as the swells were two or three feet, but when they became major waves with white caps and then begin to break over the gunwale of the lobster trawler, that was a different story.

Suddenly, to me, it became less than a user friendly body of water and I began to realize that not only was I unable to keep any helpful amount of food in my stomach, I began to experience fear that brought beads of perspiration on my head and in my armpits, even in the midst of the cold saltwater spray that washed over me.

On one of those trips out to sea, the skies suddenly and without warning, began to get dark, very dark. Swirling black clouds began to form on the horizon and soon our trawler was enveloped not only by the angry clouds, but also by the howling winds. A major "Nor'easter" began to cause the hardy and well built trawler to bounce like a small, fragile cork, tossed about mercilessly by the angry waves.

"Yo! All hands on deck!" the captain yelled. "Let's get those traps up and on board and get out of here before we get swamped."

The swells were now major waves that rocked the trawler like a rocking chair. All of us jumped into our rain gear, pulled on our rubber boots, made for the deck and grabbed hold of the wet ropes to pull in the traps in the middle of a major storm. The traps were full and heavy. Storm or no storm, they had to be pulled up onto the deck. The trawler rolled from side to side and bow to stern. The captain made every effort to keep the bow headed into the waves, but the high winds made it almost impossible to do so.

I made every effort to hang on to my part of the rope and at the same time keep from throwing up. Everyone else seemed to be handling the waves just fine. At least it looked that way to me. They were experienced lobster fishermen. I was not.

I lost footage on the slippery deck, the rope slipped out of my hand and I began to slide toward the rail flat on my back. I was terrified. About that time, the trawler shifted in the waves and I began to slide in the opposite direction. Then it shifted again and I went sliding back the other way. I felt like a fish out of water, flopping around on the deck and sliding dangerously close to the edge and over. I couldn't hear myself scream above the howling wind.

If it hadn't been for the guy next to me grabbing one of my desperately flailing arms and helping me wrap a safety rope around my waist, I probably would have wound up somewhere in the middle of the Atlantic.

After what seemed like hours, the traps were on board and the lobsters dumped in the hold. The lids were slammed shut and locked down. One by one we retreated to the safety of the cabin. At least it felt safer to me than sliding around on a wet, slimy deck. I was happy to have survived. There had been other rough seas during my short term employment on the lobster trawler, but this one had to be the roughest.

"Good work, Lee," yelled one of the crew members as we shook the water from our raingear and took off our hats.

"Thanks," I yelled back, knowing that I had not done all that much to help. I spent most of my time trying to survive.

"Yeah, you did alright out there for a land-lubber," yelled another. Pats on the back and thumbs up from others gave me a sense of accomplishment. I managed a sheepish grin because even I recognized that I wasn't much help on this one. Had it not been for my unknown rescuer, I wouldn't even have been in the cabin. I would probably have wound up as lobster feed on the bottom of the ocean. I knew at that moment that I was a boy among men.

Regardless of the much appreciated support, I still needed to find a place to throw up. I wasn't about to go back out on that slick, slimy deck. Everyone in the cabin could see my predicament so they gave me room to run. I made it to the john just in time.

Though it took several hours of strenuous effort, expert piloting and work by the captain and crew got us safely back into port. The trawler was tied up at the dock alongside other trawlers that had just returned from battling the storm at sea.

During the offloading of the lobsters I overheard a conversation that said one of the trawlers did not make it back. It was swamped, rolled and sank in the storm. The coastguard had been sent out to see if there were any survivors.

That was my first encounter with this kind of tragedy. I noticed that all of the crews from the various trawlers were deeply affected by what happened. Even though they may not have known which trawler went down or any of the crew members aboard, they knew there would be families anxiously waiting to hear news about whether it was the one on which their husband or brother or son worked.

I learned that even though these tough men may compete with each other for the best lobster grounds or for the buyers that pay the best price, they still had a sense of belonging to a special group of men who faced danger on an almost daily basis. Death at sea is tragic, even for the toughest of them.

The job on the trawler had lasted for just a month or so before the storm. I had already come to the conclusion that lobster fishing wasn't for me. The captain of the fishing fleet, who could see that I was not cut out for the lobster industry or any other business that had to do with the ocean, came to me and suggested that I might want to seek other employment.

"Lee," he said, "I don't think you're cut out for this kind of work. You handled yourself pretty well in the Nor'easter, but your inexperience also created a danger for a couple of my experienced regulars. I can't afford to lose one of them and I don't want to endanger your life either. I suggest that you find some kind of work on land that's better suited for you."

"Yeah, I guess you're right. I thought I could handle it, but when that storm hit I could tell that the ocean is not for me."

"Lee, why don't you go on back home and plan to go to school and complete your college education? I think that would be a good thing for a young fellow like you."

"Right," I agreed half heartedly, as I was scratching the back of my head. "That may not be a bad idea."

I did want to complete my education, but I had no intention of returning to Pryor in order to do it. I had left all of that behind - far behind. And I had no plans to go back, ever.

"Go on over to the office and pick up your check," he said, as he shook my hand. "Good luck in finding the right kind of job, kid."

"Kid?" I thought. *"I'm almost twenty years old and I've been on my own for almost two years and I'm still considered a kid? I*

may not be as tough as those guys on the trawler, but I've managed to survive on my own. Kid indeed!"

I walked away in somewhat of a huff over to the shack at the end of the pier that he called their office to pick up my check. As I did so, I realized *"Lee, you've just been fired."*

I also realized that whole sea adventure did make me notice one thing in addition to not planning for any future work on trawlers. Every time I went out to the Red Lobster Restaurant to eat and I saw that large glass aquarium inside the entrance with all those lobsters with green rubber bands around their claws, I had a strange feeling. Which one of them was in the traps that I had pulled on board the trawler? Were they aware of why they were in the tank? Did they get fed while they were waiting to become someone's dinner? What if I were in there and they were out here picking me out for their dinner? What would that feel like?

It was just one of those quirky little thoughts that popped into my mind when I saw them there! I don't eat at the Red Lobster very often. Lobster is not really a menu item for me.

I left the fishing industry to those who could handle it.

There was something else about the ocean that niggled in the back of my mind, but try as I would, I could not - or chose to not remember what it was.

CHAPTER 3

I did eventually find me a job on land. Over the next five years I worked at a local feed store. It was located on good solid, terra firma. I didn't have to worry about falling off the loading dock, unless, of course, we had a sizeable earthquake. Besides that, I knew more about the products provided by the store to the farmers in the area. Most of them were 'gentlemen' farmers, but their animals still needed what the store had to offer.

Even though I had sworn never to live on a farm again, I felt a certain sense of identity and kinship as I talked with the locals about what would probably work best for them on their farm and with their animals.

During those years I also managed to attend a small college where I was able to earn my Bachelor of Science degree. The college offered evening classes, which made it possible for me to attend classes while maintaining my employment at the feed store. I majored in sociology with the thought of becoming a counselor, or psychologist, or Department of Social and Health Services counselor, or a teacher, or a psychiatrist or whatever. *"At least,"* I thought, *"I will have the degree."* Now, what to do with it?

Working and attending school allowed little or no time for social activities. I had met a couple of girls who attended some of my classes and also some fellows that I enjoyed having a beer with after class, but working and attending school full time was a full time job with little time left for socializing.

I did meet a girl that I really liked and we even dated off and on during our junior and senior years. We had a very good relationship and enjoyed being together. However, when I couldn't make up my mind as to whether I wanted to be married and settle down to the grinding work schedule that I had seen on the farm or stay free to roam as I please, she decided to marry someone else.

In my youthful naiveté I thought she should have given me more time to think about it. Looking back I can now see that my indecisiveness about marriage and my insistence on giving it more time, were major factors in helping her come to her decision.

One or two other failed relationships made me decide that I would concentrate on a career and "make something of myself." I remember some individuals, especially a certain banker, back in Pryor, saying not long before I left, "Lee, you really ought to work hard, like your folks, to make something of yourself."

Well, with a lot of hard work and determination – perhaps I did learn that from my parents and grandparents on the farm. Whatever! I did "make something of myself." At least in my own mind I did.

After finishing college, I was finally employed for several years as a secretary for a very good local attorney in the larger city of Portland

"Do you have any experience working in a professional setting like a law firm? he asked, when I went in for my interview.

"No," I replied, knowing that he had already looked at my resume. "As you can see, I was raised on a farm, did odd jobs across the country, had a short stint aboard a lobster trawler and worked in a feed store while going to college. That's about it."

"Why do you think you can make it here with so little knowledge of this kind of profession?" he asked.

"Well," I replied, "frankly, I need a job. And when I heard that there was an opening for an office person with your Law Firm I decided to see if what I learned in college could be used to land me a job."

"Well," he said, "at least you're straight forward about it. I like that. Maybe we can give you a chance to use that degree you earned. I'm looking for a male legal secretary and file clerk. I do a lot of late night work and take out of town trips. I need to have a male employee to assist me in my work and accompany me on those trips.. I have no time to waste on possible sexual harassment issues, if you understand what I mean."

"Yes, sir," I replied. "I think I understand exactly what you mean" I didn't foresee any problem there! My memorable experience hitchhiking across country cemented that issue in my mind.

Attorney Holston Carter, of the Carter, Howerton and Wainright Law Firm, taught me much about the legal profession and even allowed me to sit with him in court and take notes for him during various trials. Over time I became acquainted with other attorneys, judges and counselors. I found out that my degree in sociology actually had some benefits as we interviewed clients and prepared for cases in court.

I never attended Law school, therefore I never did become a "full-fledged," real life attorney. I often acted like one, though, as we entered and left the courtrooms. I had a leather briefcase and wore a double breasted suit with a silk tie.

In time I became known as a "paralegal." I couldn't decide whether that meant I was a 'semi-attorney,' or an 'imitation attorney' or an 'almost attorney.' In any case, I enjoyed looking like one. I enjoyed the work and looked forward to the various issues that we had to face in the office and courtroom.

Since I had no family responsibilities, other than for myself, I was able to save money over a period of time and make a down payment on a small condo, not far from the waterfront where I could look out over the ocean. Look at it? Yes! Ride on it? No!

Life was beginning to look pretty good. I even bought me a car. Not that I needed one, for Portland had all the ready public transportation that was needed to get around the city. A bus took me to within half a block of the attorney's office where I worked. And when we had to go out of town, I would ride with Holston Carter in his sleek Porsche.

However, it just seemed that a man who had been on his own for twelve years and now nearing thirty years of age should have a car. I had been driving the farm vehicles since I was about twelve. All I would need is some refresher practice and I would be good as new.

So I bought a BMW convertible, bright red with white leather interior and chrome spoke wheels. It set in a rented garage most of the time, but I would take it for a drive along the coast on the days that I didn't have to work – which were very few. There was always some research to be done for the next court case.

That was my routine for the next several years. It wasn't a particularly exciting life, but I really wasn't all that interested in excitement. I had determined to "make something of myself," and so invested all my time, energy and financial resources into accomplishing that very thing. I could think of no other purpose for doing it than the statement made by that banker in Pryor, "Lee, you really ought to make something of yourself."

Single, now just past forty, a condo paid for, a substantial bank account and another BMW – a third one, this time bright blue with soft tan leather interior with chrome spoke wheels. Things were looking pretty good and if he could see me now he would know that I had "made something of myself." It felt good! My life may have been dull by some other people's standards, but I was successful in my own eyes.

Then I began having that interminable nightmare! After finally seeing the face of my dad in it, I could do nothing else but try to discover what it meant.

Like it or not, I had to go back.

CHAPTER 4

Somehow, after all these years, I knew Pryor would be different, but I never expected it to be this different. I felt like I was driving into the twilight zone, a ghost town in the middle of the night.

I had been gone for almost twenty five years, having no contact with those I had left behind. I probably left for all the wrong reasons, but at the age of eighteen, at least for me, it did not take much to formulate a reason, good or bad.

I kept asking myself, "Who needs a reason? Just do it because you want to do it! You're eighteen years old. You don't have to explain your decisions to anyone. Your life is your own! Go out there and make something of yourself."

I grew up like a lot of other kids living in that area. We all worked in the fields for we were raised in a farming community.

My parents were hard working farmers like all the other people around. My dad drank a lot and my mom seemed to put up with it because she loved him. At least she said so.

We lived on the same farm that had been occupied by my grandparents, my great grandparents and, I was told, purchased and developed by my great-great grandparents. The land and buildings had been in the family for at least four generations.

Nevertheless, even though I had some enjoyable times on the farm, I remembered that even at an early age I did not want to spend the rest of my life on a tractor plowing fields or in a barn milking cows. I wanted to "see the world." I needed to "find myself" and be "my own person." At least those were some of the reasons for my leaving that I told to myself.

I could not be content at being just another predictable branch on the Edward's family tree with a predictable occupation, farming, in a predictable small town, Pryor, with predictable community activities – school plays, church on Sunday, community pot-lucks, county fair, community Christmas tree, community gossip and all the other stuff that often pervades a small farming community.

The fact that my father had a major drinking problem with alcohol and treated my mother less than kind on occasion probably also played a major part in my leaving when I did. At least, that is another reason that I filed away in my mind to refer to in those times when I began to question why I had made the decision to run away in the first place.

There were other reasons, I was sure, but I had buried them for so long, I could not force myself to bring them to the surface. I had tried it before. It was too painful so I pushed them even deeper into my sub-conscious mind.

Twenty five years! Almost a whole generation! And now I am faced with the fact that I am being driven by an inner compulsion to come to a place that I had long since put out of my mind as being a place of worth in my life. Here I am following that nightmare and wondering what other kind of nightmare I might be getting myself into.

It had been a long and tiring trip across the country from where I lived in Portland, Maine to the Midwest and Pryor, the place of my birth.

It was late at night when I arrived in Pryor and it occurred to me once again what an unusual name for a town. I always thought that maybe it was named that because it was prior to something that someone expected to happen in that place, or perhaps prior to naming it something else. Maybe it was prior to being nearly blown off the map by a tornado that passed through it when I was a kid.

I still remember seeing the flat under side of those dark, ominous, greenish colored clouds that blocked out the sun. The green, my dad told me, was the tornadic winds sucking all the pollen from the trees and ground up into the air. It was really eerie! It was almost dark as midnight in the middle of the day. Everything was still as death. Even the chickens were aware that something was about to happen and they went racing for the chicken house, clucking and cackling.

The cows and horses also made effort to find a place to hide. The milking barn was their place of refuge and I could see the cows coming at a rapid pace in a long black and white line from out in the open pasture. Our dog, Old True, sought shelter between my dad's legs. It seemed that all the eyes of every two-legged and four-legged farm animal were glued on the dark and foreboding sky.

I remember that my dad, mom and I ran to the barn where the last of the animals had sought refuge.

"Shut the barn doors and fasten the windows," my dad yelled. And so we hurriedly shut and secured all the barn doors. The wind was so strong that it was difficult to stand and even more difficult to hear my dad yelling to tell us what to do.

Finally everything was closed and boarded up and dad yelled for us to head back to the house. "They may get blown away if the tornado makes a direct hit on our place, but they will otherwise be in out of the wind and blowing debris."

We had just reached the steps to our front porch when it began. A small funnel dropped down out of the angry, black clouds. I remember that I imagined it to look like the inside of one of those cotton candy machines that I, as a boy, had seen at the county fair. Someone would hold a paper cone and move it around inside the container, gathering up the sugar mixture that was spinning out from the sides like a spider web. Little by little the cone would gather more sugar mixture until it became a full sized cotton candy. I was always mesmerized watching them make those cotton candies.

This was totally different! Here the clouds began to swirl around the funnel like a massive spider web, only they weren't pretty pink and white cotton candy. They were dark and ominous and threatening. This cotton candy was black and dirty! The clouds were deadly! The roar of the wind was deafening!

Then, what appeared and sounded like a frightening sucking sound began to reach from the ground to the clouds. All the stillness in the air was blown away as what sounded like a dozen freight trains sped across the horizon. The funnel touched down. The earth and everything in the tornado's path was being ripped apart or pulled up by the roots and flung against the sky.

My parents and I stood on the front porch of the farmhouse and felt the force of the wind that spun around the parameter of the tornado. It touched down just beyond the town of Pryor, two miles away. We saw the roofs of houses, assorted pieces of cars and machinery and whole trees – as well as helpless animals, flying through the air.

I remember my dad yelling above the howling wind, "Let's get inside and down in the basement. No telling which direction that thing is going to go. No need standing out here and getting blown away. We've done everything we can do. Let's just pray that the animals are safe and that we don't all get killed."

We rushed to get to the basement and to possible safety. The old dog beat us to it. He was there first. We could hear our farmhouse creaking and groaning as it was being beaten and battered by the gale force winds. I began to wonder if it would be destroyed and we would all indeed be blown away or, like my dad said, get killed.

I was really afraid. The more the wind blew and things were crashing against the side of the house, I began to cry.

About that time the power went out in the house and the basement was totally dark. I found myself groping through the darkness to find my parents. Soon, I felt my dad's strong arms embracing me and my mom and, with trembling voice, trying to reassure us that everything was going to be alright.

"It's going to be alright, son, he said. "Don't be afraid. I know it sounds awful, but we'll just ask God to protect us and everything will be okay. Shhhhh."

Come to think of it, I had forgotten all about that. I don't remember my dad ever mentioning that we should pray about anything. I also believe it was the only time that I can remember my dad ever made a move to hold me and reassure me that I was going to be alright. He was never much for showing any kind of tenderness or affection to either mom or me.

It seemed like an eternity, but eventually the howling wind subsided and everything became deathly still once again. We waited for another period of time before my dad indicated that it would probably be alright to leave the basement and check to see what, if anything, was left standing.

We walked back up the basement stairs and out on to what was left of the front porch. We discovered that the old farmhouse had weathered the storm.   It still stood strong, proud and sturdy. Nothing had been damaged beyond repair. However, large trees were uprooted and limbs had been blown up against the side of the house, damaging siding and breaking windows.   Many of the shingles had been blown from one side of the roof and most of the front porch was gone.

We walked through the yard, now filled with limbs and debris, to check the barn where the animals had sought refuge. Everything seemed to be standing, except for a large segment of the barn roof that felt the force of the wind. It lay out in the pasture. Upon entering the barn we were confronted by some very frightened animals that needed the familiar sound of our voices to calm them down.

I remember we walked through the barn talking to the horses and cows, telling them that everything is okay.   Even thinking back on it sounds a little strange to be attempting to sooth the frightened animals by telling them that everything is going to be okay, as if they could know what we were saying. Nevertheless, they seemed to understand because none of them made effort to back away when we put our arms around some of their necks or patted them on the rump. I think they were just glad to hear the familiar sounds of our voices.

That tornado made quite an impression on me as a kid. It cut a massive scar across Mother Nature's face that took several years to heal. The town was still being rebuilt from the aftermath of that tornado about the time I had decided to run away.

I do know that the experience of seeing and feeling that tornado made quite a scar on me. There was a time when I, as a kid, loved to stand on our big front porch and watch the sound and light shows, as I called them, move across the prairie. The huge, billowing, white thunder clouds would form and I could hear the roll of thunder. It was always deep and powerful, sometimes shaking the house and porch on which I stood.

I can remember my mother telling me that the angels were having a bowling game and the pins were being knocked over. That's what made the sound of thunder. Then the lightening would strike, sending a blinding streak from heaven to earth. I stood in awe. Mom would then say, "One of them made a strike!"

I don't know where she got her information, but as a kid, it sounded reasonable to me. I had yet to learn of hot and cold air clashing in the atmosphere or the sudden discharge of electricity between clouds and earth. Angels bowling and making strikes tickled my imagination.

However, the tornado dispelled any sense of standing on my front porch and enjoying a sound and light show. It felt more like some evil monster that decided to march across the land and destroy anything and everything that got in its way. I always lived with the thought, and fear, that maybe it would decide to come back and finish what it hadn't accomplished on the first pass through.

Maybe that was part of the reason I decided to leave Pryor.

CHAPTER 5

As I arrived from Portland and drove through town looking for a possible place to spend the night, once again it occurred to me that perhaps it was named Pryor, prior to disappearing off the face of the earth as a town. It appeared to me that it was almost like a ghost town with few stores apparently still functioning and what appeared to be other stores boarded up or torn down altogether. And yet, the population sign at the city limits stated otherwise.

I had to remember that it was a rural town at night, not like a city with eternal daytime because of its streetlights. Not everything would be visible and not everything would be the same as I remembered it.

Nevertheless, it looked nothing like the bustling community away from which I walked twenty five years ago. Back then it was alive with several stores, gas stations, churches, schools, cafes and even one or two fairly decent restaurants. The streets were sometimes lined with cars, pickups or trucks – well, what few people had them. Then they were all parked at an angle to the curb.

I remember that there was even a flashing yellow traffic light at the main intersection of town – a true sign of a developing community. But that was years ago and I was just a high school kid.

Things had changed and evidently not necessarily for the better. However, I had to remind myself again that it was night time and I probably couldn't get a good picture of what it really looked like until day light.

I did manage to find a small motel with perhaps a dozen rooms and a red, neon welcome sign that flashed "Vacancy." I checked in, determined to get a good night's sleep before setting out the next day in an effort to discover my purpose for being here. There was no one to phone that I had arrived, so, after checking in, I took a good hot shower and settled into the old and bumpy-mattress bed for some sleep.

Just as I was drifting off to sleep I heard a voice – or was it just a loud thought that sounded like a voice? Whatever it was, it was clear enough to cause me to sit upright in bed. I immediately thought that I was about to experience that nightmare once again. However, this time I knew I was wide awake when I heard, *"I'm glad you came. I have been dreaming and hoping and praying that you would."*

What was that? I felt like I was hearing voices. I had heard about people hearing voices. What I had heard was that it was not always positive. Hearing voices could be the sign of some degree of mental illness. Whatever, I was convinced in my mind that I had heard a voice. Sleep came slowly and it didn't stay for very long periods of time. I tossed and turned throughout the night.

When I awoke, the sun was already high in the sky and the day was warming up with the possibility of being a scorcher. I knew that I had a lot to do – whatever it was, and I wanted to get it done as quickly as possible. I wanted to get back to the city and my work. Holston Carter was reluctant in the first place to give me a week off to take care of "family business" and I was hoping it could be accomplished – whatever it was that needed to be accomplished, in that brief period of time.

I did not tell him that I was following the urging of a nightmare. He might not have been so generous in allowing me to be away for a week. But, had it not been for that, I would have still been happily involved in my work.

Well, that is probably an overstatement. I was *somewhat* happily involved in my work, plus my personal relationships were somewhat lacking and those I had were somewhat strained. Nevertheless, true or not, I would be in my own condo in Portland – not here in a second rate motel in Pryor.

I knew what I had to do first. I had to visit the home place, if it still existed after all these years. It was only a short distance out of town, perhaps a mile or two. I couldn't remember exactly. I just knew that when I was a boy I could see the top of the grain elevators from our place.

I climbed out of bed and did a few stretching exercises that I had been doing on a regular basis to maintain a healthy body and a good physique. The shower sputtered and spewed water and air until it finally decided that it would pour forth water. It took awhile for the hot water to find its way to the showerhead. The shower had obviously not been used in quite some time. After showering, shaving and getting cleaned up for the day I decided that I would try to find a place to have some breakfast.

I walked out into what was a beautiful, clear sunlit morning. The air was still. Birds were in great voice as they sang their various melodious songs. Even though I had not slept well, I felt good.

When I went to reserve my room for another night, I was warmly greeted by the person at the desk

"Good morning, sir."

"Good morning to you," I replied.

"I hope you had a pleasant sleep last night."

"Yes, I slept," I said. I didn't tell her that it was in short periods of time, off and on and for what reason. I could have told her they needed new mattresses on their bed, but that wasn't the reason I couldn't sleep.

"I believe I will be staying another night. Is it possible to reserve the room for one more night?"

"It most certainly is. Shall I leave the charges on the same credit card?"
"Yes, that will be fine, thank you."

"Have a nice day," she said, as I exited the motel office.

"Thank you," I replied, "And I hope that your day is a nice one also." I wasn't sure what awaited me in my day. I hoped that it would be a nice one.

As I pulled out from the motel I noticed that my car needed gas so I searched for a service station and finally found an old 76 station at the edge of town that also housed a small convenience store. After filling the gas tank, I went inside to pay for the gas and purchase a few items that I thought I might need, or my parents might need, since I was coming in unannounced and they would have an extra mouth to feed for a day or two.

The kindly older gentleman behind the counter had a welcoming smile and said, "Good morning, sir. Welcome to Pryor. Are you new in town?"

He had probably noticed the out of state license plate on the BMW convertible parked outside. I had long since forgotten that in smaller towns everyone knows when a stranger comes into town and registers at a local motel – probably the only one to register in a week or perhaps a month.

I told him "Yes, I am new in town. But I used to live here as a boy. I notice that things have changed some since then."

That seemed to trigger his interest and he began to ask questions.

"You used to live here, huh?"

"Yes, I lived here but left when I was eighteen."

"Did your family live here then?"

It seemed like a no brainer question, but I said, "Yes," my parents, grandparents and great grandparents lived here and on the same farm."

"And what were their names?"

"Their name is Edwards."

"You are the Edward's boy?"

"Yes, I am the Edward's boy, Lee Edwards. C.J. and Melissa are my parents."

"Well, I'll be a….." he exclaimed as he hit himself up beside the head with the heel of his hand. My name is Ben Robertson, a long-time friend and business acquaintance of your family. I knew you when you were just a little tyke and also when you were in high school."

He came around the counter, grabbed my hand and began to pump my arm as though he were trying to bring up water from a well. "It is so good to see you after all these years. We were all wondering what ever happened to you and if you were still alive."

"I'm alive," I said. I couldn't think of anything else to say, but it appeared obvious that I was alive.

He finally quit pumping my arm. Then in a kindly, soft, paternal type voice Ben said, "Son, I guess you already know about what has happened to your dad and your mom."

"No, we've been out of touch for a lot of years."

"Well, then, you may not have heard that about five or six years ago now your father was killed in an automobile accident."

"No, I wasn't aware of that. How did it happen?"

Inwardly I was thinking that he probably had gotten drunk like he had on many occasions and ran his car into someone else and killed both of them. It seems like more and more innocent people were getting killed by drunk drivers. We saw that all the time in court. Some drinking fellow would drive when he shouldn't have, run a stop sign and maim or kill a whole family without ever being aware of what he had done.

Little wonder that organizations like Mothers Against Drunk Driving [MADD] are mad and on the warpath against that kind of thoughtless and careless use of alcohol and the privilege of driving. I sometimes wondered why the state sold liquor and then the state troopers turned right around and arrested the person who bought booze at their store. Seems like a no brainer to me.

Nevertheless, I asked again, "How did it happen?"

"Well, Lee, your dad was one of the finest citizens this community ever had and we all miss him terribly. When you left, it did something to CJ. It seemed like he just lost heart for awhile and lost interest in farming. You know, of course, that he was hoping that you would take over the place from him, just as he had done from his father?"

Before I could respond, he continued, "Well several years later, when the farm began to fail, like so many others around here, it was another terrible shock for C.J. His drinking became worse and worse until one day he must have realized he was getting nowhere fast so he sought help. Some of us friends pooled what little resources we could get together and helped him go through alcohol rehabilitation. He took the long course, not the outpatient treatment.

"He came out with a new determination to make something of his life. At the same time your mom began taking care of a woman and her baby while he was gone to rehabilitation. When he got back he sold a few acres of land off the farm. He invested in a small feed store here in town and helped to keep other farmers from folding by making sure they had seed grain to sow He carried them on his ledger until they could sell their crops and could repay him. Yes, he is really missed by a lot of us who are left in the community."

Something inside me was actually pleased to hear that my dad had done something decent in his life and contributed to the welfare of others. He probably did several decent things, but in my rebellious teenage years I had seemed to remember only his drinking problem.

However, Ben had not answered my question, "How did the accident happen?"

"Well, one night CJ and Ron were coming back from delivering some food and seed grain to one of the families out in the country. Their children and the father were all sick with the flu.

CJ heard about it and loaded up some groceries and medicine to take out to them. On the way back some fellow ran a stop sign, crashed into the driver's side of CJ's old pickup truck and he was killed instantly. Ron was in the hospital for several days and still walks with the help of a cane.

"The fellow in the vehicle that hit them must have come off without a scratch," he continued. "The Sheriff said that the guy must have been on a drunken binge or maybe he and his wife had been fighting. Either way, he was drunk or he was mad. He just ran the stop sign as if it wasn't even there, then backed off and took off. It was a hit and run. He's never been found, even after all this time."

"Yeah," I said, "drunk drivers are a real scourge on society.

I don't think I heard all of what Ben was trying to tell me until my mind finally clicked in to what he was actually saying. I suddenly realized that his account of the accident that killed my dad was a virtual replica of the recurring nightmare that I had experienced for endless months. My mind spun in circles as I tried to fathom what it could possibly mean.

Not yet fully able to comprehend it, I changed the subject.

"By the way, who is this Ron fellow that you mentioned was with my dad in the wreck?"

"Well, Lee...." I noticed he spoke hesitantly, "Ron is a young man that your folks took in when he was a boy. He had a single mom that really struggled to make a go of it here in town. As I seem to remember it, she was a junior or senior in high school when she became pregnant. She never did tell who the father was. We all had our suspicions, but none of us knew for sure.

"When her folks found out about it they became enraged. They were teachers in the high school and to have their daughter pregnant caused them a lot of grief. Finally, they sent her somewhere to live with an aunt or someone until the baby was born. I don't know if she ever finished school.

"She and her baby, Ronald, eventually came back to Pryor to be with her folks, but I guess the hurt was too deep between her and them. They never acknowledged the baby as their grandchild. She tried to make it on her own by working over at Tony's café, but it was really difficult. Folks in Pryor, good as they are, seem to be able to forgive but they have a hard time forgetting, especially when someone does something that offends their moral principles.

"Anyhow, your folks saw what was happening to her and the baby, so they took them in at the farm and provided for them. Your mom looked after Ronnie a lot while his mom worked.

"Some people in town were unkind in speaking about what your folks did They felt that somehow they were not respecting the girl's parents. That didn't matter to them. They saw a woman and baby in need so they pitched in to help out. They treated them like family, and I guess they were good company for your mother while C.J. was in rehabilitation.

"Are these folks still around town?" I asked, for whatever reason I couldn't say. The question just kind of "came out."

"Well," answered Ben, "Ron's mother married a truck driver fellow who stopped by the café those times when he passed through Pryor. After awhile they got to know each other and he asked her to marry him. He knew that she already had a small son. At first that didn't seem to be an issue, but talk was, after they had a child of their own he decided he really didn't want the boy around because he wasn't his.

"Ron's mother talked to your folks and they took him back in to live with them. Ronnie felt right at home because he had lived there for so long. His mom and step-dad moved out of town. I don't remember where they went. Your folks raised Ron from the time he was a young kid, maybe four or five, and taught him how to work on the farm. As he grew up he seemed to be a great help to them. At least to hear C.J. tell it he was. He has been with them ever since, maybe twenty years or so. He must be about twenty four or five years old now."

"How about my mom?" I asked.

"An amazing woman, Lee," he said. "She has to be one of the most, uh, what's the word, 'stalwart?' Nah, too bland! She was a Rock of Gibraltar! She was a true helpmate to your father. Even when he was going through his own personal hell, she was there encouraging him, praying for him, holding him up and doing all those things that were necessary to bring him back from the brink of self-destruction.

"At the same time she was making every effort to be a good wife to your dad, she was also working at being a mother, or better perhaps, more like a grand-mother, to Ron.

"She had her own personal grief when you left and it took her a long time to regain her desire to continuing living, but she knew she had to for the sake of your father and the boy and the place they both loved."

"Mr. Robertson, are you implying that I am the reason for the difficulties my mom and dad were having? I can't accept responsibility for my parents' problems. You don't know the circumstances surrounding my leaving and I can't see where you have a right to pass judgment on me for what I did."

I was more than a little upset by the implications of what he had said.

"Now, Lee, calm down. I wasn't trying to judge you or do any such thing to imply that you caused all their problems. You asked me about them and I just wanted you to know how your leaving had impacted their lives. They loved you then and they have loved you through all these years, even though they did not know where you were or what had happened to you.

"I will have to say, however, that when several of us who are their close friends saw them going through their grief and personal hells, we had our own thoughts about a young man who would put his parents - and some others, through what they went through and never bother to be in touch. And, I'll have to tell you, those thoughts were not always kind.

"We found some truth in the statement that time heals all wounds. However that may be, we found that with time the pain can be dulled and deadened by other circumstances that come along to demand our time and energy. I think that is what happened with all of us. In time we quit caring about you, forgot about you and went on with our own lives."

I had already paid for the gas, so I picked up the few supplies I had purchased and headed for the door, feeling a mixture of anger, frustration and not a little guilt. However, at the door I had to turn and ask the question again, "What about my mom? Where is she? Is she still out on the farm?"

He said, "No, Lee, Melissa no longer lives on the farm. She is a resident in the Mary and Martha Nursing home where she has been for about two years. That's a place located at the south end of town. I don't think it was here before you....before," he said. "She has not been doing very well, especially since CJ died and Ron was injured so badly."

"Thanks," I said, then turned and walked out the door to my car, thinking, *"I will go to Mary and Martha Nursing Home and find out for myself what her condition is."*

CHAPTER 6

"Lee Edwards?" the woman at the reception desk asked.

"Yes, I have come to see Melissa Edwards, my mother."

"Your mother is in room 102," she said, "but I think you need to know what to expect when you go to see her."

"What to expect?" I asked. "Why? Is there something wrong?" Even I could realize that it was a stupid question as I asked it. Of course something is wrong or she wouldn't be here in this place.

"How long has it been since you have visited with your mother?"

She must know that I had not been to see her since she arrived at the nursing home, so I said, "It has been several years since I have had opportunity to come visit her. I live in another part of the country."

"Well, however long it has been she is not the same person you may have remembered from the last time you saw her. She has been with us about two years. In that time her health has broken, especially since the loss of her husband in a car accident, and she has suffered a stroke.

"She now experiences impaired awareness and rarely responds to our voices. She is almost completely immobile and must receive constant care. Her condition worsens each day. I thought you needed to know this prior to seeing your mother."

I thought, "There it is again. Prior! Everything in this town, even its name, is prior to something. Perhaps in this case it is prior to my mother's demise after I get to see her – or her shock from seeing me."

When I walked down the hall to room 102 a strange sense of loneliness welled up inside me. Why?   I thought I had it all together.

I gently and slowly pushed open the door to the room, not knowing what to expect as I looked at my mother for the first time in about twenty five years. She lay there, with an almost angelic look on her delicate, wrinkled face. Her eyes were closed. She was very frail and not at all as I remembered her. She was then a healthy, robust woman, able to drive the tractor and ride the horses with the best of them.

Her caregivers had obviously fixed her hair that morning, and made her very comfortable in a clean bed with clean surroundings. Her hands were folded over her breasts as though she were praying.

I stepped up to the side of her bed, took hold of the rails and stood gazing down at her for long, silent moments. I took a deep breath and said, in a subdued voice,

"Hi mom."

Somehow the words had difficulty coming out because I had not said "mom" in many years. It was almost like a foreign word spoken to a complete stranger. And yet, I choked up a little even as I spoke it.

Opening her eyes ever so slightly, she looked up at me for the longest time, as if thinking whether what she saw was real. "Lee?" she whispered. "Lee? Oh, Lee, I have been dreaming and hoping and praying that you would come, and you did." She lifted her frail and gnarled hand to touch mine.

With a slight smile and nod of her head, she closed her eyes once again and immediately relaxed into a deep sleep with a beatific smile on her face. I just stood there. Looking! Wondering! And with a feeling welling up inside that I had not felt for a long time - maybe never.

Sorrow? Sorrow for sure. It flooded in on me like a raging river as various memories flooded through the corridors of my remorseful mind! Regret? I suddenly regretted all the wasted years that I had failed to contact this beautiful mother that I had willfully closed out of my life and heart. Sense of failure? For sure! I had failed. I failed to be there at a time when they needed their son, because their son was too busy thinking about himself and running away.

I just stood in silence for awhile, then pulled a chair up beside the bed and sat down. .I reached through the metal railing to hold her worn and wrinkled hand, gently caressing it, so as not to awaken her from her peaceful slumber. There was so much I wanted to say. At least I think I wanted to say it, but I didn't even know where to start. It had been twenty five years.

"Mom." Nothing more would come.

CHAPTER 7

As I stopped and opened the gate and came onto the old farmland and viewed what lay before me, my heart was saddened – somewhat like that of having had a beautiful dream that had never been realized. Suddenly all the memories of my childhood and teenage years flooded back in on me.

I drove through the open gate and up the long dirt lane that led to the farm house. I parked my car in front of the house, got out and walked up to stand and gaze at its weathered beauty. The place was not quite as I remembered it, but after all these years, someone had kept it in fairly good repair. It had lost much of its stately appearance, at least in my memory from my youth.

After standing and carefully looking at it for awhile, I sat down on the big porch steps and looked out over the meadow and toward the town of Pryor that lay about two miles away. Looking back from the perspective of an adult I could now understand why this farm was such a special place to my parents and to their parents before them.

I looked out over the fields and remembered that, as a boy of ten or twelve, my grandparents would come each spring to visit and stay to help on the farm. It was always a special time for me. Grandpa loved to have me sit beside him on the tractor as he helped my dad plow the fields that lay to the South and West of the house. Dad always planted corn – like grandpa before him.

He said corn was his favorite crop because he loved the fragrance of the tassel and silk, especially after a long hot summer day when the evening breeze moved across the fields.

Somehow I knew that it was also his favorite crop because I remember them talking about the fact that corn brought a good price and produced income for the year ahead. I came to realize that both dad and grandpa were romantics as well as realists.

During those times, grandma and mom kept the massive house spotless. I seemed to remember that she dusted everything every day until the furniture shined until you could see your face in it. The curtains and drapes on the high windows were always neatly pleated and open to let in the bright sunlight.

I loved to stretch out in the middle of the living room floor and watch the flecks of dust - what few there were left after grandma's meticulous dusting, float around in the rays of sunshine that came through the windows. I tried to catch the illusive flecks on the tips of my fingers. I finally discovered that if I licked my finger first, the dust would stick.

Both women loved to cook. Every meal consisted of delicious, mouthwatering food and always with plenty of milk to drink, coming from the moderate size dairy herd we had. My parents also sold milk to the local creamery and the people of Pryor enjoyed the bounty that came from the Edward's dairy farm. I always wondered what people in Pryor did prior to getting milk from our farm.

In addition to cows I remember that we had a few horses that I loved to ride along with my mother.

"Lee," she would say, especially in those times when she found me in a rebellious mood, "how about you and me saddling up a couple of the horses and ride down and see how the cows are doing?"

"Aw, mom," I would whine, "can't those old cows look after themselves for once?"

"C'mon, son," she would cajole, "it'll do you good and, besides, the horses need to be ridden.   We can do two things at once, ride the horses and check on the cows."

"Actually," I thought, *"it would do three things. In addition to checking on the cows and giving the horses their exercise, she could get me out of the house and doing something constructive instead of whining and messing up everyone's day."*

I loved to ride horses with my mom. She was good at it an could ride like the wind. She could ride without so much as a hint of a bounce in the saddle. I often found myself bouncing up and down like someone riding on a trampoline. Yet, it was always a good time when she suggested that we ride. It made me feel really important to know that my mom wanted me to go for a ride with her.

I guess I must have been too busy thinking about myself these past years to remember how special the times were with my mom.

We also had some chickens and a couple of geese that could have used an attitude adjustment. They were always on the prowl for the family dog, Old True, because he would never back off when they came honking and hissing at him.

He withstood their challenge and neither side budged an inch until one or the other of them got weary of the standoff and wandered away looking for something more interesting to do.

The memories raced back across my mind as I sat there looking into the past. I could see myself racing with Old True. He was a mixed breed, shaggy haired, lop-eared dog that had wandered onto our place and suddenly discovered home. No one ever knew where he came from. We just assumed that someone probably dropped him off at the end of our lane, leading up to our house. We never saw any signs in town announcing that a dog had been lost. Of course, looking at Old True, one could understand why no signs were ever posted for his return.

All it took was one bite of bread that dad tossed to this starving animal and there was instant bonding. That mangy old dog never left his side. I figured that is how he got his name. He had found a place to live – and ultimately die. True to the end!

After that squatter dog got settled in and made our place his home, he followed my dad everywhere he went. Whether dad was sober or drunk, Old True stuck to him like glue. He rode with him to town in the pickup. As soon as dad headed for the pickup the dog began to jump and wag his crooked tail and give a bark that spooked the cattle that grazed nearby. He didn't seem to mind dad's drunk driving. That old dog himself acted like he was drunk about half the time.

Looking back now, I can remember that there were times when I wished that I could have ridden with them, but I never liked to be around my dad when he had been drinking. When I saw him that way and he appeared to be getting ready to go somewhere in his car, I would find a reason to be doing something else around the place. I got into such a habit of avoiding him when he was drunk that as I grew up I never bothered to ask if I could go along with him when he was sober.

The dog didn't mind his drinking at all. When someone in town would make a comment like, "CJ, that sure is a mangy looking

51

mutt you have there." Dad would reply, "That's true." He never denied it, for he was indeed a mangy looking mutt.

He would sit beside dad on the tractor as dad plowed the ground, making it ready for planting. I remember that I would sometimes ride with my dad on the tractor when I was younger. But now, as a teenager, there wasn't room in the seat for both Old True and me. When anyone saw the two of them on the tractor they would wave and comment, "That old dog sure loves to ride with you, doesn't he, CJ." Dad would reply, "That's true, he sure does."

When dad would feed and water the cows and bring them in for milking, Old True was right beside him. His very presence – with shaggy, multi-colored hair, crooked tail curved over his back and one ear flopped over an eye, must have been the only thing that encouraged any wayward cow to fall in line. It sure wasn't his stately and ferocious manner, except maybe for the bark. He walked beside dad as if he were boss of the roundup, looking up at dad for approval with adoring eyes and a long tongue hanging out of the side of his mouth.

I remember that there was a time when I stood and watched the two of them and thought that I would have enjoyed helping my dad drive the cattle into the barn for milking. However, Old True did a better job of it – and probably followed orders better. After Old True showed up, I can't remember that dad ever asked me to help with getting the cows in for milking.

I would watch Old True sit by my dad's swing on the front porch and have his head patted and shoulders rubbed for what seemed like endless hours. When a visitor dropped by and saw them setting like that they would often comment, "CJ, you two look like you're from the same litter." Dad would reply, "That's true, we could well be."

One time Mr. Olson, a neighbor from down the road, dropped by with his sleek, magnificent German Shepherd and began telling my dad about all the great qualities of the Shepherd breed and how useful they are around the farm as guard dogs and how obedient his Shepherd is. He commented that dad's old dog looked like he didn't do much for he surely didn't look like much."

I remembered my dad saying, "That's very true. About all he does is go into town with me and keep any car thieves away from my pickup while I'm in the store" - as if there were any car thieves in Pryor. There were hardly any cars in Pryor at the time.

"However," he continued, "he also helps me plow the fields and get them ready for planting. And too, he brings in the cows for feed and water and milking. But better than that, he sets beside my swing on the porch and lets me keep my hands busy by rubbing him on the head. Yep, it's true. He isn't much to look at, but he's true."

Dad's attitude toward that mangy old dog played a major part of why we all came to call the dog Old True.

In spite of it all, and whatever I may have thought about my competition for dad's attention with that mangy old dog, Old True and I used to run like the wind out across the meadow, through the rows of corn, past the herd of cows and down to the lake where gaggles of geese and ducks seemed always to be present in abundance. Old True loved to help them take flight. They were more cooperative than the two, long-necked radical, independent rebels that stayed up by the house.

When Old True died – from old age I guess for we never really knew how old he was when he adopted us, I can remember that it hit my dad pretty hard. He really lost a true friend. I don't think I had ever seen my dad cry before.

I don't know if I cried because dad did or if I cried because Old True was dead. Either way it just seemed like it was kind of a crying time. We all sat around in silence for the longest time just crying. I think we all felt like we had lost a member of the family.

Even now, setting here on these steps and thinking about it, I can feel a lump welling up inside my chest and throat. That ugly old dog just wiggled and slobbered his way into all our hearts.

Dad buried Old True out under the shade tree outside the kitchen and back porch. He used to lay there whenever dad wasn't around. He liked to stretch out there because the two cantankerous geese also liked to squat there and I think he did it just so they couldn't. I can't remember ever seeing the geese under the tree again after it became Old True's burial place. I think they knew somehow that Old True was a permanent resident and they should stay their distance and find another place to squat.

The farm property had a good lake down by the back pasture. It was a very good place to fish, for at that time, twenty or thirty years ago, it seemed to have plenty of fish just waiting to be caught. I was always glad to proudly display my "catch" of fish and my mother would prepare the two or three perch for supper, pretending that it was a mighty fine bunch of fish. She would tell me every time that my catch would be plenty for the whole family. I noticed she always had another meat dish on the table, just in case.

The lake was also a good place to swim in the heat of the summer. After helping dad and grandpa do the chores we would all head down to the lake for a swim, to "cool down," as they would say.

We had other "hands" to help out with the farm work, as dad hired some of the people in town to help with the milking, harvesting and other things that needed to be done. But when grandpa was there, he acted as if I was the only one that could really help him. I felt almost grownup when Grandpa was around, even though I was probably only ten or twelve.

Memories flooded in as I sat there on those steps and recalled the times and the people I left behind, who lived here and loved the land. I began to wonder why I had ever left. The 'reasons' I once laid claim to began to seem less and less valid or important.

My mind recaptured those few moments at mom's bedside, *"Lee. I have been dreaming and hoping and praying that you would come, and you did."* It was all so surreal! Those are the very words I heard in the motel when I first arrived in Pryor.

I got up from the steps where I had been seated, stepped a little ways out into the yard, turned and took a long look at the house. I couldn't help but wonder what all had happened in those intervening years since I had left to "go find myself" and to "make something of myself."

"House, If only you could talk. What stories I'll bet you could tell me."

I heard from somewhere, perhaps from within my own mind or conscience, *"Whenever you are ready, I'll tell you!"*

CHAPTER 8

It was quite an elaborate house for being a farmhouse. Built in the 1800s, the house stood as an imposing structure not far from what was once a bustling, boom-town. It was built in a time when lumber products were cheap. The wood had been shipped in from somewhere where forests of massive trees had produced the kind of wood grain that was perfect for this kind of building. The old house was once a truly magnificent specimen of what man could do with the right kind of wood.

It stood three stories tall with a large basement. Dormers balanced delicately on the roof. A pillared porch embraced three sides of the structure. Gingerbread woodwork decorated the porch rails, the eves of the house and the casing of each of the forty windows – sixteen on each floor and eight in the dormers. Indeed, it was once a magnificent structure testifying to the creative and construction genius of men.

It was now time to take inventory of what was once a grand house, now apparently much less so, but not totally falling apart as I had imagined earlier. Someone had worked to keep it in an acceptable state of repair. Since Ben had told me that Ron occupied the house, I prepared to knock on the front door.

As I lifted my hand to knock, I heard a vehicle moving up the graveled lane to the house. I turned around to see who it might be.

Ben Robertson exited from his pickup, waved at me and walked up the walkway to the porch. I was surprised to see him.

"Hello, Lee," he said as he began to climb up the front steps. "Just thought I would drive out to see how things are going and if you needed any help with anything."

"No, I don't think so. I was just setting here thinking some about the place and getting ready to knock on the door to see if I can go inside to look around. As you said earlier, Ron still lives here, so thought I'd better knock."

"Yes he is still living here and he's making every effort to take care of it as best he can.

"However, Lee, I really came out here because I want to apologize to you for maybe having said something that sounded like I was judging you earlier today. I really didn't mean for it to sound that way but I guess it did. I want you to know....

"Don't worry about it, Mr. Robertson. I guess I had some of it coming after staying away all these years and not letting anyone know where I was – especially my folks."

"Your mother and father have been the backbone of this community for years. They always looked out for others before they looked out for themselves. That's partly why, when your dad was killed and your mother placed in the nursing home, several of us have taken on the task of trying to help Ron keep this place in fairly good repair. We want to do it until that time if and when they ever needed to sell it to get money to take care of their needs. We haven't always done our best, but at least we want you to know several of us have tried."

"Thank you, Ben," I said. "And I truly mean it. I was wondering why it didn't look like a total disaster as I had imagined it might be after all these years. There doesn't appear to be any sign of vandalism or anything of that sort."

"Actually," Ben said, "we did have some boys try to break out some windows one time when they thought no one was here, but they were caught and soundly dealt with. Since then no one has bothered to trespass because everyone, including the kids, knows the whole town is very possessive of that which belongs to your parents and will protect it at all costs."

"You all obviously do think highly of my parents by doing this for them for so long."

"We just figured it was our way of saying "thanks" to your folks for all they did for all of us when they were able.

"Well, I had better get along and let you have your time with the house. Ron should be around here somewhere. Maybe down by the barn. I haven't seen him in town today. See you later."

"Thanks Ben," I said. "I look forward to talking with you again."

Ben walked back to his pickup, started the engine, waved and started off back down the lane toward Pryor. It kind of looked like the times when dad would do the same, only difference was Old True wasn't sitting in the passenger seat with his head out the window and his crooked ears flapping in the wind.

I turned back toward the door, took a step forward and was greeted by the man I presumed to be Ron. "Hello. Would you like to come in?" He asked. "I was standing by the door when I heard you talking with Ben."

He invited me inside, but not before I noticed that he walked with a distinct limp and used a cane. I presumed that it was the result of the accident that Ben Robertson had told me about, the one in which my dad was killed.

"My name is Ron, Ron Edwards," he offered as he reached out to shake my hand. "And your name is?"

"My name is Lee Ed...Lee Edwards." I'm the son of CJ and Melissa Edwards."

I didn't catch any indication that he was surprised that our last names were the same. Yet, all the while I was wondering how he had the same last name as I did. I thought that, maybe since he had been living with them all these years, my folks may have adopted him when his step-dad didn't want him.

I continued, "I grew up here when I was a boy, but have been away for a long time. I just wanted to come back to see the place and check on the folks."

"Come on in," he invited. "I've also lived here since I was a boy, like several others that grandma and grandpa sort of 'adopted.'"

When inside, he waved his hand around toward the interior and said, "I apologize for not having the place really clean. A single fellow trying to keep up this size place, plus doing the chores and work related to it, keeps me fairly busy. I'm really grateful for the help of some of the people in town. What I really need is a good wife like Gran Edwards who always kept it sparkling. There don't seem to be any like her left in Pryor.

"You're welcome to look around if you want," he said. "Take all the time you like. I can show you around the place if you want me to but I suppose you would just rather wander through on your own."

"I won't be interfering with what you're doing, will I, if I just take a look around? I don't want to impose."

"No, you're not interfering or imposing. Take all the time you want. Go into any part of the house you want. There's nothing you can hurt or is off-limits. Just make yourself t'home."

"Thank you, Ron. I appreciate you're kindness in letting me, a total stranger, wander through your home."

"No problem, Lee. After all, it was your home at one time. So just take your time and stay as long as you want. Okay?"

"Okay. Thank you."

I couldn't help but notice his dark sparkling eyes, the rustic tanned face and the unruly, curly black hair that appeared to rebel against staying in place. His smile was infectious and even though he limped, he had a strong, muscular body that showed the fruit of hard work.

When we shook hands his grip gave evidence to the fact that he had not spent a lot of time in the kitchen washing dishes or sweeping the floors. It felt like he probably spent more time milking the cows or throwing bales of hay over the fence for the other animals to feed on.

We stood just inside the large entryway and I began to drink in memories from so long ago. Those memories now began to come back as stark realities before me, some pleasant, but not all.

Ron must have noticed that I had exited into my mind and became lost in my thoughts, so he simply stepped toward the living room, leaned against a doorway, crossed his arms and let me explore my memories in personal solitude.

The first floor consisted of a grand entry through double, leaded glass front doors that stood ten feet tall. The doors and the glass were still intact, though the glass was clouded over with a little dust and dirt. *"What single man has time to wash windows in the front door?"* I thought. The doors opened to reveal the curved stairway that led to the second floor.

I remember that, as a kid, I would start at the top of the rail and slide backwards all the way to the bottom post - preferably without my parents knowing about it. Dad didn't want me to "mess up" or put a scratch on the beautiful woodwork that great-great grandpa so painstakingly created. I don't remember him ever suggesting that I might hurt myself.

Nevertheless I had a great time flying down that rail. That is, until I got caught at it more than once and my pants were hot and not from sliding on the rail. Still, before I left home at eighteen, I boldly slid down that rail right in front of my dad – more as an act of rebellion than to get in one last slide. I found myself smiling an impish smile just thinking about it. Dad wasn't all that impressed.

"You really liked to do that, didn't you?"

I looked around, thinking that someone else had followed me into the house that may have known what I did then, or was reading my mind. No one was there, except Ron, who was still leaning against the door into the living room. He was looking the other way and then walked into another part of the house. Maybe it was just my thoughts coming to the surface.

"Well, yes I did like to do that. Even as a kid I had to work, sometimes from sunup to sundown in order to help keep the farm going. And I had other things I wanted to do."

I hadn't realized that I had actually spoken aloud to the thought until I heard my voice echo in the big entryway.

"Things like what?"

"What do you mean, like what?" I said, "Like, having some time to hang around with other kids my age. Being an "only child" is not all that it's cracked up to be. It seemed like my folks expected me to act like an adult when I was still a kid and then when I did become an adult they treated me like a kid."

"Lee," I thought to myself, *"you've got to quit talking to yourself."* I shook my head, took a deep breath and walked over to where Ron had been previously standing. He wasn't there.

The living room lay to the right of the foyer and once contained grand period furniture that my great-great grandfather had shipped in from some far country that excelled in such workmanship. It had also housed a grand piano whose music, it is said, "could be heard all the way into town." The piano was a prized possession. It was now covered with a quilt. From all indications, no one played on it anymore.

Except for a few scattered pieces that were being used, the remaining furniture was covered with assorted blankets to protect them from gathering dust. I could see what Ben meant when he said they had tried to help Ron keep the place fixed up. The town's folk had not only been busy helping work the land but also to protect the house and the furniture within it.

As I stood and looked around the room, the floodgates of my memories were opened wide.

"Remember how you used to sit at that piano and play? Just about every day you found time to play. You were born with an ear for music and you brought joy into this place as the sound went from basement to attic."

Caught again by the surprise of hearing a voice other than my own, I spoke in muffled tones, "Who are you? Who else is in this house?"

"No one. Just you, Lee. When you stood out front awhile ago you said that if only this house could talk it could tell you a lot of stories. What do you want to hear? It has lots of stories to tell because it has seen a lot of things about which to tell."

"I must be losing my mind. This whole thing has just about stressed me out. Now I'm hearing voices. Next thing I know I'll wind up in that nursing home with my mom or else in a mental ward somewhere."

I thought for just a fleeting moment that I would head for the front door and get outside. But on second thought....

*"No, I'm not losing your mind. I'm searching for answers. This house can help me find them. I'm a grown man and I'm not taken in by foolish thoughts of strange voices. It's just that everywhere I look I am reminded of things that happened a long time ago. It really **is** like the house talking to me, in a way."*

So I took a long breath, shook my head to clear the cobwebs, and determined that I would continue looking through the rest of the house. At the same time I found myself looking over my shoulder.

To the left lay the library that once contained literary works of people like Aristotle, Plato, Chaucer, Shakespeare and other great philosophers and poets from around the world. I remember my mother and grandmother reading some of that ancient wisdom and I sat – sometimes restlessly but always intrigued, and listened.

This is where I sat and listened to the stories about the sea and the grand exploratory adventures of Captain Cook and

Columbus' discovery of America. I had to grin as I remembered that it was much more pleasant to listen to the adventures than to ride the waves in the middle of a hurricane. I had to laugh out loud at the boyish desire for such an adventure when I heard and read the stories in this quiet library compared to rolling around on a fishing trawler's slippery deck and yelling for my life.

There were times when I wondered how these classics found their way into a farm house library way out in the middle of nowhere. My parents always reminded me of the hunger for education and reading that was instilled in my grandparents by my great grandparents. When they travelled to other places, they always brought books back for the library.

Many of the books were now missing and the shelves that once held those grand works seemed to be sagging just a bit and some of the polish had long since disappeared. But the room still contained an atmosphere of adventure about it. It kept entering into my thoughts that this is the place where I read and heard the reading of some of the great historical works and adventure tales that quicken the hearts of young boys and men alike. It feels almost like a sacred place. A quiet hush embraced the room as my eyes scanned the remaining books that contained many stories, now unread.

I had to wonder, did these captivating stories play a part in my wanting to go "see the world?" Perhaps. I know that I used to imagine being on a daring safari in Africa, hunting the elephant or the great lion, then I would grab my cardboard sword and go creeping around the yard looking for the creatures of the great Savannah. Old True never appreciated the jousting episodes or being considered as the lion in the Savannah.

If not there, then I would be riding the waves on the high seas, going in search of treasures in foreign ports, or escaping a band of brigands who made every effort to rob me of my treasures. It came to me that imagining sailing on the high seas and actually doing it while trapping lobster off the coast of Maine were two entirely different things. I didn't get seasick reading about the adventures on the high seas.

I learned a lot from my folks as I was growing up here in this room. I recall that sometimes they would look up from the book they were reading and say things like, "Son, a person should never think of themselves more highly than they ought to think, but should always think with sober judgment."

I thought for a long time that meant that you should be sober and not drunk, like my dad, when you talk about yourself. However, they said that I should be realistic and not brag on myself or, conversely, put myself down. They had a lot of practical wisdom.

I had certainly spent a number of years thinking more highly of myself that I should have - especially when I had the idea that I might be too good to work on a farm all my life, like my parents. I also spent considerable time putting myself down and not thinking very highly of myself for the way I treated people, especially my parents, when I ran away. I found it difficult to have sober judgment.

Walking around this great room I began to run my hands along the edge of the bookshelves and that of the library table that lay covered with a bed sheet in the center of the room.

Suddenly memories flooded in like a tsunami. *"Remember how you once imagined the freedom that must lie in the foreign ports or the great cities? In addition to the school homework you did at this table you would daydream of walking among people in other lands and helping those in trouble in other cities? Do you remember? Of course you do. Was that one of the reasons why you felt you had to leave here?*

"I really don't know the reasons why I chose to leave," I said. out loud.

"If it was not to escape a father you thought was uncaring or insensitive to your needs or a small town that was too confining and too gossipy, then perhaps it was because of a sense of adventure that was resident in your heart. Could it be that you were only following the dream that was in your heart, right?"

Could it be true? Could that possibly be the reason for me leaving? It was good to think of that possibility. However, it seemed that it was something else; something far less noble or heroic.

A very large kitchen, dining area and what was once a master bedroom, occupied the remainder of the downstairs. Somewhere in the intervening years either grandpa or great grandpa had determined to add an indoor 'outhouse,' tucked in the area under the stairwell and accessed from the dining area. It was still there but had been "modernized" into a very nice bathroom.

The kitchen had the usual cupboards, sink and counter. The large table that used to set in the middle of the room was no longer there. The space was a lonely reminder of a great day when this part of the house was basking in the fragrance of bread baking in the oven and delicious, aromatic food spread on the large table, around which sat family and hired hands, talking and laughing and eating.

Silence! No laughter and no voices were now to be heard, only a steady breeze finding its way among the limbs of the lone oak tree that served as the headstone for what was once Old True's final resting place. There was kind of an eerie loneliness that swept across me as I stood gazing first at the empty kitchen then out to the lone oak tree. It sort of reminded me of myself – suddenly alone, very lonely and very empty.

Why did I leave? I keep asking myself that question, but the answer continues to elude me.

The second floor consisted of five bedrooms and one - later added bathroom. Each room was reached by a single hallway that ran from one end of the floor to the other, having a window at each end.

My bedroom was at one end of the hallway. I remember that my parents slept in a bedroom at the other end of the hall because they knew I was afraid of the idea of being on the second floor all by myself while they slept in the master bedroom on the first floor.

At first that was reassuring, because I was a little kid. But then as I grew older and into my teen years, I was upset that they thought they still had to sleep upstairs. They could have moved back into their room on the first floor, but for some reason, known only to them, they didn't.

I walked down the long hallway to my old bedroom door, a little hesitant about opening it. It might be the room where Ron sleeps. Where *was* Ron? I probably shouldn't be wandering around through the house like this. He really doesn't know me. I called his name, "Ron! Oh, Ron!" but didn't hear an answer, so I opened the door and walked into the room.

CHAPTER 9

As soon as I opened the door, it squeaked a little. Then I remembered something long forgotten. When I slept in that room and began to have some nightmares I was glad my folks were nearby in their upstairs bedroom. I never told them that.

Even looking into the room caused unwelcome panoramic memories to come flooding back. They were palpable! It seemed like almost every night when I was going to sleep I would experience three shadowy figures coming out from under my bed.

"Remember the shadowy figures that plagued your sleep?"

I just about jumped out of my skin. "Of course I remember. I have long since tried to forget it but standing here in this room makes it all come back. It's like it is happening all over again and just as real now as it was then."

I remained standing by the open door. I could still see in my mind those figures, only they weren't figures like people, but three wide, ribbon-like, flowing things that came from under my bed and entered into my body. I guess that's where they went because they would flow into bed with me and disappear. I would wake up in the blackness of the night in the room, terrified and sweating, wanting to call out to my parents, but so scared that I had not voice.

What am I saying? I'm a grown man and I don't believe in ghosts or demons or all that dark stuff. It was just a kid's imagination playing tricks and running away with him.

"Was it?"

"Of course it was. I can see that now."

"Then why are you afraid now? Why is your heart and pulse racing? Just the thought of what happened in this room all those years ago still causes you to be afraid. You were here when it happened then and you know how you reacted to their presence."

My heart was racing, my pulse pounding in my ears and drops of sweat formed on my forehead. It is broad daylight, sun is shining in through the windows and here I stand shaking like I did when I was a kid when my room was pitch black.

Suddenly three words came into my mind and, attached to each of those words, was one of those shadowy, ribbon-like "figures." They each had a name. I could not name them then, but now I can. Fear! Lust! Anger!

Fear! That one was easy. I was scared out of my wits much of the time when I was growing up on the farm. I never really liked to be by myself. I liked to be with my dad or grandpa or that old dog or someone.

I always wondered why it was so terrifying for me to "go check on the chickens," like mom used to say. "Lee, go check on the chickens and see if they are in the garden," she would tell me. The chickens *always* seemed to be in the garden and the garden was way out on the other side of the barn, a long way from the house. Why did those damn , miserable, scrawny chickens always have to be in the garden?

Looking back, I think dad and mom realized I was having trouble with being afraid. Maybe that is why they slept upstairs or kept sending me on errands around the farm to help me get over the fear. Sometimes I thought I had it conquered. Nevertheless, it seemed like every night that same shadowy figure would come out from under my bed and trigger the fear all over again.

Standing there in the doorway to what used to be my room I realized that that fear had never really left me. I think I have tried to run away from it, but somehow it keeps following me, even as an adult.

I fear for my job. I fear for my future. I have a fear of failure in my work. I fear for my health and even my life. I was afraid in the car with the old man that picked me up when I was hitchhiking. I was afraid out on the ocean on the lobster trawler. Now that I stop to think about it, fear just seems to permeate everything about me.

I used to hear my mom humming a tune as she walked around the kitchen preparing a meal or cleaning up after one. In the middle of her humming she would sometimes make little statements like "Perfect Love drives out fear," or, "You know you can't control that which you fear."

As I look back on it I believe she was aware of my presence in the room and was trying to plant a message or idea in my mind that would help me get over my fear. I don't' think it worked.

Lust! There wasn't anything particularly strange about that. Every boy experiences some form of lust, especially when his hormones begin to kick in and his body starts to develop from a little kid to a young man. I don't think I had any more problem with that than did my friends in Jr. high and high school. We always had our little inside jokes about certain girls in school and wondering what it would be like to...well.

There was always one of the guys bragging about his "conquests," but we all knew it was just talk. Most of us couldn't work up the courage to ask a girl to go to a school dance or to a movie, much less get involved in something like sex.

The lust seemed to be mostly in our imagination, or like some would say, "In your dreams." It certainly was only in mine. Or was it?

Still, there is that nagging feeling in the back of my mind that it had to do with more than my imagination. The more I tried to shake it, the more it pressed hard to find its way to the front of my consciousness. Then it crashed through and demanded a hearing.

A narrow stairway led from the hallway to the upper attic. My mother used to encourage me to go play in the attic because it was a quiet and private place and I could spread out my toys and not have to pick them up. She said it was a bright cheerful place and I would love it.

She did not know that I was afraid to go into the attic. I imagined all kinds of ghosts and creatures inhabiting the space and would do awful things to me were I to venture into their domain. I cannot remember ever having gone into the attic alone from the time I learned to walk until the day I walked away from this house. At least that is how I chose to remember it.

As an adult I could now go into that attic and see for myself what there was that made me so afraid at the time. I opened the hallway door and began to climb the steep stairs. The sun was shining through the dormer windows and cast a soft light on the dusty floor and few boxes and pieces of furniture that had been stored there.

"Remember the girl?"

"What girl?" I asked aloud.

"The girl you really liked. She was one class behind you in high school. You were both in the school chorus and sang together for school concerts. You were in band together and marched at the football games. You remember, don't you? She really liked you and you would invite her over and show her around the farm and ride horses with her and run with her and Old True through the rows of corn. Sometimes you would retreat to this attic. You do remember, don't you?"

"Yeah," I said, rather hesitantly. "I kind of remember her now that I think about it. Her name was Betty. No! Billy Jo. No! I can't remember. It's been a long time ago."

"You used to sing about her when you weren't with her. "My Bonnie lies over the ocean. My Bonnie lies over the sea. Oh, bring back my Bonnie to me."

"Now, I do remember. Sure, her name was Bonnie. Bonnie Shoemaker. I had forgotten all about her."

Actually I had not forgotten about her, I had just chosen to not remember her. But suddenly it all came back and much clearer than I cared to remember. It happened here in this room, this attic that I never wanted to be in again. This is where lust came boiling to the surface and took control of my will and my emotions.

She told me to stop because we really shouldn't' be doing what we were doing, but desire won out and I couldn't stop. I kept telling myself and insisting to her that it was love that I had for her that made me do it. Now I know it really wasn't love, it was lust, pure and simple.

Well, it certainly wasn't pure and it wasn't simple. I did something that I later regretted and then came to realize that it played a major part in ruining both our lives. And, come to think of it, it was probably the main reason that made me decide to run away from home in the first place.

Bonnie avoided me at school. I also avoided her and acted like she was nobody, though I really did like her a lot and even thought that I loved her. Even my buddies began to question me about what had happened between us. They noticed that we were avoiding each other.

"Did you have a fight? Did you break up?" they would ask.

"None of your damned business. What we did doesn't concern any of you." I would yell at them.

One day Bonnie met me at the end of the hall by the lockers. She had waited until no one else was around. She dropped the bombshell. "I'm pregnant. And it's because of what we did in the attic of your house. I haven't told anyone else, not even my parents. I don't know what to do and I'm afraid. .What should we do, Lee?"

"Oh, for crying out loud!" I shouted in anger, then turned around to see if any of my classmates had heard me. Bonnie, began to cry. I just stood and looked at her in disbelief. I didn't know what to say. We were both at fault. But I couldn't, or wouldn't, accept the responsibility and began to rationalize: maybe it wasn't mine.

"Are you sure it's mine?" I asked her. I knew it was the wrong thing to ask even as the words came bursting out of my mouth.

She looked at me as though I had slapped her in the face and accused her of being with someone else.

Then I suggested that maybe she should abort it. And I told her so. "Why don't you abort it and you won't have to worry about it. No one will ever know."

She was devastated. I was in such a state of shock and fear of what everyone would say if they knew, I didn't know what to do. I knew I wasn't ready to be a father.

Bonnie's parents were both well-liked and respected teachers at the school. Her mom taught Home Economics and her dad was the band director. When it became apparent that she was pregnant, talk began to spread like wildfire through the school. Little huddles of fellows as well as girls began to surmise who the father might be. Teachers were trying to deal with the gossip and do what they could to give some kind of support to Bonnie. It was obvious that her parents were embarrassed - and furious.

Then Bonnie just disappeared. She no longer attended classes and everyone began to question what had happened to her. Her parents simply said that Bonnie had chosen to go live with family members in another state in order to finish her schooling.

That did not stop the gossip about what kind of a guy would get a girl pregnant so that she could not finish school or be a part of a graduating class or attend school dances or have a boyfriend that did not treat her like that.

For some reason all eyes seemed to look at me and all fingers point at me because everyone knew that Bonnie and I had spent time together in classes at school and also at the farm. I became very angry. I was angry at the guys that snickered and mimicked, "We know who the father is! We know who the father is!"

Things changed around home also. My mom and dad remarked that I had become sullen and "not like my old self."

"What is the matter?" they would ask.

"Nothing," I would yell, and walk out of the room, go to my room and slam the door.

I wasn't telling the truth, of course. I lied. Everything was the matter! I didn't pay attention when I was a little kid when mom told me, "Lee, always tell the truth and then you won't have to remember what you said." Or, "Know the truth and the truth will set you free."

Standing there in the middle of that attic room, I realized that I have been lying and slamming doors ever since. I have been slamming the door on my memory of the way I treated Bonnie. I slammed the door on my relationship with my father and mother. I slammed the door on the relationships I had tried to develop with other women.

I had slammed the door on anything that had to do with my past and jeopardized my future in the process. In reality, I had slammed the door on myself. I had lived with the assumption that I ran away from home to "find myself." In reality, I couldn't run away from me.

Now, looking back at it, the reason I ran away was not to find myself, but to lose myself - to lose myself in an anonymous environment where no one knew me and, in reality, I didn't even want to know myself. Shame and anger go a long way in helping to destroy a person and I was well on my way to destruction.

What was that other thing that mom used to say while she was humming around the house? Oh, yes. Following one of my angry outbursts I would later hear her saying just loudly enough for me to hear, "The thief comes to steal, kill and destroy." And then she would say something about not letting the sun go down on your anger.

My anger had surely acted like a thief, stealing and destroying what could have been a lot of good relationships and I certainly had not gotten rid of my anger before the sun went down. There have been many sunsets since anger took root in my life.

Mom also managed to counsel me about living a life that counted for something. She called it "abundant life." Oh, I had an abundance of stuff back in my condo, a job as a paralegal, and a BMW convertible, but abundant life? Hardly!

"Hello. Hello. Are you up there, Lee?"

It was Ron calling to see if I was still in the house.

"Yes, Ron. I'm still up here. I will be right down."

I descended the stairs from the attic, closed the door, instead of slamming it, and walked back down the circular staircase that led to the main floor. Ron was standing at the bottom of the stairs waiting for me.

"Are you alright?" he asked

"Why? Don't I look alright?"

"Sure, I guess so. I was just wondering if maybe some of the memories of this place had overwhelmed you a little. You have been upstairs for quite a while. I just wanted to let you know that I have to feed the livestock now and will be out at the barn. If you want to stay longer that's okay. Just wanted to let you know where I will be."

"Thanks, Ron. Thanks for letting me look through the house. It's getting late. I guess I had better get on back into town." And, I thought, *"get ready to go on back home to Portland in the morning."*

As I pulled my car out to the head of the lane I could see Ron headed toward the barn, leaning heavily on his cane and walking with a distinct limp. This farm is quite a responsibility for a young man with a major physical disability

CHAPTER 10

I stopped by Ben's convenience store to pick up a couple of items before returning to the motel. He seemed to be loaded with questions.

"How did you find things out at the farm?"

"Actually, Ben, things look in real good shape."

"Do you think it looks the same as it did when you lived there as a boy?

"Well, not quite, but it is pretty much the same, except a little weather worn."

"Are you pleased with the way the towns' folks have helped to take care of it?"

"Actually all of you have done a great job keeping the place up."

"What did I think of Ron?"

His last question appeared to have more personal interest for him than the earlier ones.

"Ron seems like a fine young man."

"He is a fine young man. Ron has lived with your dad and mom practically all of his life but they never really adopted him. He began using their name when he went to school. I think it was because of his mother and what was said about her.

"Your folks just asked the school board if Ron could use their name on his school records and they said that, under the circumstances, it would be okay. They knew that the Shoemaker name might be an embarrassment to Bonnie's parents in the school system. They are good teachers even though I personally think they dealt with Bonnie's situation in a less than positive way. They never could accept Ron as their only grandson."

"Bonnie," I thought. *"Of course. There was only one Bonnie Shoemaker in the Pryor school system. There it is again. Pryor! She was the only one in school named Bonnie, prior to getting pregnant and prior to leaving to go somewhere else to have her – or was it, **our** baby? Is Ron my son?"*

"Ben," I asked, "how do you come to know so much about my folks' business and this thing with Ron and all the other things with the school board?"

"Well, Lee, I happen not only to own this gas station and convenience store, I have also acted as mayor of Pryor for several years, I was on the school board when you were here in school and I am an attorney and just happen to be the one that has drawn up your parents will. I am in a position to know all about them without being a part of the town's information sharing system and community weather channel."

He continued, almost as if reading my planned intention to return to Portland as quickly as possible, "Lee, I think it would be a good idea if you stayed around town for awhile, at least until you find out what will happen with your mother. And too, you have some legal responsibilities related to the farm. There are decisions to be made that Ron will not be able to make, relative to the disposal of the property, if that is ever necessary. I need to tell you that you are the only heir to the farm.

"But," I protested, "I have a job to get back to and bills to pay. I can't earn a living while setting around here waiting for something to happen."

"I can understand that," Ben replied, "but someone has to make some difficult decisions and, as their one and only son, at this point in time your name is at the top of the list."

"I'll have to think about it," I said, as I picked up my purchases and exited the store.

Walking back to my car I thought, "The very place I wanted to get away from and now...No! It wasn't the *place* I was running from, it was what I did in the place. It wasn't the place or the peoples' fault, it was mine. But now, I'm stuck between the proverbial rock and hard place. What do I do now?

~~~~~~~~~

Back at the motel the phone conversation with my boss in Portland did not go all that well. I had been gone for almost a week and his work was piling up and he needed my help and there were depositions to be handled and case research to be done and on and on. I suddenly had the feeling that if I did not show up soon I could well be looking for other employment. I really did not want to lose that job.

At my age I could not afford to be fired and begin seeking other employment. I didn't know how to do anything else; I had never done anything else except fish for lobsters and some other odd jobs. Well, I did do some farming when I was a kid but that was a lot of years ago. I really needed to keep that job. It gave me a good income, health benefits, a future and eventually, a comfortable retirement. I had to go back to work in Portland, and do it right away.

At the same time it was beginning to look like the new demands on my life here in Pryor were looming larger and larger. It was too far to commute, except by private jet, one of which I did not have.

I needed a little more time. How much, I don't know, but at least another week. Perhaps I could get Ben – since he is an attorney, to contact my boss and explain to him the situation with which I am confronted and, attorney to attorney, there could be something worked out.

Who am I kidding? That's not for him to do. I have to make a decision and either way it won't be an easy one with which to live. Of course, the one I made to leave home when I was eighteen was not an easy one with which to live either. And too, I have made a lot of other decisions along the way that were not easy to live with.

Suddenly the old fears began to float up to the surface of my conscious mind. What if I lost that job? What would I do? What if I can't sell the condo? What will I do with the farm? A lot of "what ifs" began to take over my thinking.

I needed to go somewhere and think.

Sleep didn't come that night when it was supposed to so I lay there with a thousand thoughts running through my mind and none of them coming to any order. I remember my mom used to say something like, "Now Lee, you take every though captive until you can get it in order before you speak it."

Well, I couldn't capture the thoughts much less get them in order. So I just wrestled with the covers until somehow I fell asleep. I don't know where the thoughts went.

It seems like a person has to sleep fast here in Pryor. That was a short night and it is morning already.

Even though the night was short, somewhere in the middle of it the myriad of thoughts must have gotten lost in the dark. My mind came to a decision on its own because I awoke knowing what I had to do. I knew I had to go back out to the farm and over to the lake. That had always been my "thinking place," even when I was a kid. The lake!

By the time I showered, shaved and ate breakfast, the sun was already high in the sky. It was warm enough to put down the top on the car. It was something I always enjoyed because I loved to feel the wind and hear the chirping of birds – even the city birds, as well as all the other noises of the city. Today it would be the country birds and very little traffic noise.

Somehow I felt a peace within me about what must be done. Where it came from I don't know, but I'm not going to knock it.

For some reason, known only to God I suppose, I decided to stop by Ben's store on the way. I didn't need to let him know where I was going, but he had said something that niggled around in my mind.

"Good morning, Ben," I said, as I stepped into the front door of his convenience store.

"Oh, hi, Lee," he replied as he finished giving change to one of his customers and wish him well with the decisions he had to make. I overheard him say to the 'thirty-something' young man, "You'll make the right decision. You have a good head on your shoulders and you will be able to live with the decision you make without apologizing to anyone for making it."

The fellow said, "Thank you, Ben. That means an awful lot to me coming from you. I'll spend some time thinking about it and let you know what I decide, Okay?"

"You bet, it's okay," replied Ben. "I'll be eager to hear what you choose to do."

With that the man walked toward the door with a smile on his face. Our eyes met and I found myself simply nodding my head, not only to acknowledge his presence, but to agree with Ben, and smiling at him as he left the store. Ben, I concluded, in addition to everything else, is evidently also the town counselor and psychologist.

I walked over to the counter across from where Ben was standing. "Ben, you made a statement yesterday that aroused my curiosity. As I remember, you said something about some decisions that had to be made about the farm and since I was the one and only son of my folks, *at this point in time* my name was at the head of the list.

"Did you have something in mind when you remarked that "at this point" my name is at the head of the list? Is there some other point I don't know about when my name will not be at the head of the list or was that just a casual comment on your part?"

"Well," said Ben, "you heard correctly. I told you that I am the one that worked with your parents to draw up their will and I know what is in it. I also told you that it was your dad's desire for you to take over the farm the same way in which he had taken it over from your grandfather. That has been his desire all these years."

"Yes," I said, "I remember you telling me that."

"However," he continued, "about a year before he was killed, CJ came in to see me to talk about their will. At that time he said that he had not heard from you in twenty years and it was time to do some thinking about the future of the farm. Since Ron had been living with them since he was a little kid and had become like a grandson to them, they decided that they would change the will to give it to Ron. However, they wanted to wait another five years before that part of the will would take effect.

"The will now reads that when Ron turns twenty five and if they haven't heard from you by then, the farm is to belong to Ron. The deed is to be made out in his name.

"It also reads that if you do happen to be in touch with the family before Ron is twenty five, the original will remains in effect. No matter how much your dad loved Ron, he never lost his desire that his son inherit the farm that was developed by your great-great grandfather and passed down through the family to you.

After a slight hesitation he continued, "You need to know, however, that within a very few weeks Ron will be twenty five."

I really did not know how to respond to this bit of news. It took me by surprise. What surprised me was not so much that dad had decided to put Ron in the will, he raised him; but that he kept me in it after all these years and after the way I had treated both him and mom. I just stood there staring at Ben and wondering what to say.

Finally, "Ben, does Ron know about being in the will and about the farm going to him if I'm not in the picture?"

"No Lee, I don't think he does, unless your dad told him. I have never talked with him about it."

"Thank you, Ben," I said as I turned and walked toward the door.

Now I know that I have to get out to the lake and do some thinking. First, though, I have to stop by and see how mom is doing.

CHAPTER 11

Room 102, wasn't it? Yes, that was it, so I bypassed the nurse's station and turned down the corridor to the room. When I pushed the door open I looked in on an empty bed. It had been made up and the room completely cleaned as if no one had ever occupied it, or that it was being prepared for someone else.

For some reason a sudden, chilling feeling of loss swept over me and instant anger popped to the surface. I thought, *"Why didn't someone get in touch with me to let me know about her passing? They knew I was in town and they knew where I would be staying. I'm going to have a word with whoever is in charge and give them a piece of my mind."*

I whipped around to head toward the nurse's station to talk with the person in charge and just about knocked Nurse Nancy over. She was standing directly behind me. She could obviously detect the kind of mood I was in by the expression on my face..

"Mr. Edwards," she said very calmly, "I can see that you are upset. Is it because your mother is not in her room?"

"What happened?" I barked, "Why didn't someone let me know?"

"Mr. Edwards," she said, still calm and still smiling, "Let you know what? We weren't aware that we should be in touch with you about what happened. It's just part of the thing we do for our residents. We simply moved your mother to a better room and now she is down in physical therapy for her morning session with the therapist

"Mr. Edwards, may I call you Lee?"

"Yes, that's alright. You may call me Lee. I'm really sorry about....." I was suddenly embarrassed by my less than polite, verbal assault on her. I found myself speechless.

"We have noticed a remarkable change in your mother over the past couple of days. She has been eating without us prompting her to do so. Her speech has improved some and she has even begun to form recognizable sentences without us asking several times, 'Honey, what did you say?'

"We have noticed her smiling more. She has even made effort to get out of bed and take a few steps. But, of course, we won't let her do that unless we have a person on each side of her.

"That's interesting," I said, because I didn't know what else to say.

" Interesting is certainly a good word for it." she said. "The staff is simply amazed at her progress. Suddenly it is as though she has discovered a reason for living. I think that we all noticed and agreed that the change happened following your visit with her a couple of days ago. Whatever you said or did, or whatever happened between you, evidently triggered something within her that gave her new hope or a new will to live. She is different. Come on. I'll take you over to the therapy room and you can see for yourself."

I just stood there, numb! "Nurse," I said to her as she started to lead me toward the therapy room, "Nurse Nancy, please stop." She stopped and looked back at me quizzically.

"Mr. Edwards, Lee, my name is not Nancy, it is Nora."

"Well, Nurse Nora," I continued as we stood there in the middle of the hallway, "you know that prior to my visit the other day I haven't been to see my mom in the two years she has been here. In fact, you need to know that I haven't been to see either my father or mother in almost twenty five years.

"When you tell me that my one visit has caused somewhat of a miracle to happen in her life, I find that hard to believe, considering the way I have treated them. I'm having a hard time right now dealing with that and I'm not sure I can look my mother in the face and handle the guilt over what I have done by the way I have treated them."

"Lee, parents have a way of forgiving and forgetting. Whatever you did in the past is between you and whoever. But, with your mom, just to have seen you and hear your voice must have wiped out all that. She learned that you were still alive. That must have answered a great question that she needed answered. Come on, let's go see what she's up to today."

I reluctantly and nervously followed along behind Nurse Nora as we proceeded to the therapy room and looked in on my mother and her physical therapist.

"Melissa, you are one remarkable woman today," said the young, handsome male therapist. "First thing you know you will be running circles around this room and I'll have to be careful to stay out of your way before you tackle me." His teasing smile worked its charm on mom.

"Da...vid. You'...d be...tt....er wa....tch....o..t.   Iiiii mi...t ta...kle you toooday." The room broke into an uproar with the dozen or so people laughing and clapping hands. I think I could detect mom's left foot trying to dance a little. I had been told that her right one was affected by the stroke.

Mom looked up and saw me standing in the doorway. Our eyes met and all I could do was stand there and gaze across the room into her beautiful, weary dark eyes – and cry! I really didn't care if the staff, or Nora or mom, saw it.

I wanted so much to say, "Mom, I am so very sorry for the way I have treated you all these years. I am so sorry that you and dad had to have a substitute son because your real one was so arrogant and self-centered that he had to do his own thing and couldn't see the hurt he caused his parents."

I really wanted to say that, but all I could do at the time was walk over to her and embrace the frail body that she had become and let my heart speak for me. I must have had an emotional stroke of some sort. I was now the one who could not put two intelligible words together in one intelligible sentence.

Following the therapy session the staff placed mom outside in the shade of a covered patio. The honeysuckle vine was dressed in multitudes of fragrant blossoms. The warm morning breeze gently touched each of the blossoms and sent the fragrance directly to my mom. She breathed in the aroma, held it for a long moment, and after exhaling she smiled and said, "Leeee, Do...n't yuuuu jus lo....ve hon....ey...kle?"

"Yes, mom, I love honeysuckle." I especially loved it now that I was sitting beside my mother, remembering how very special she was when I was growing up. Always the positive one! Always the encouraging one! Always the 'little sermons in a sentence' one! While at the same time always the 'dare you to not listen to me and you're dead' one! She could wield a switch or a broom handle, as swiftly as anyone.

It was so good to be setting here in the shade with her, sniffing honeysuckle, and remembering, at least, what little part of my life I had spent in her presence.

"Mrs. Edwards," called Nora, "it's time for lunch. Why don't you invite your son to stay and have lunch with you. We have plenty of room and plenty of food."

"Lillee, woo...ld you sta.... f lu....nch?" she asked as she placed her thin and gnarled fingers on the back of my hand.

I was tempted to excuse myself because I knew I had to get out to the lake and do some serious thinking before deciding when to go back to Portland to resume my job. However, looking into mom's pleading eyes, I said, "Mom, I was hoping you would ask me. I can't think of anything I would rather be doing than having lunch with you."

Following a very pleasant time at the table attempting to carry on a conversation with both of us at a loss for words. I watched as her once strong hands, now fragile and with gnarled fingers, tried to place small amounts of food in her mouth.

"Here, mom, let me help." I reached across the table, gently took the spoon from her shaking hand, and fed her, all the while remembering the many times she had cut up my food and fed me when I was a little kid. I suddenly realized that my hand was shaking almost as much as hers. We both laughed as I missed her mouth and some of the mashed potatoes fell into her lap.

We were informed that it was time for mom to return to her room for her afternoon rest. She had been up more today than she had been in months. The weariness had begun to show in the way she began to slump in her chair at the table.

"She is now in room 120," said Nurse Nora as we began to walk toward the dining room door. It's just down the other hall from where she was before and it's closer to the nurse's station and also the therapy and dining room. We thought it would be better and easier for her."

I walked with them to the room and watched as they helped her crawl into her bed and get settled in for her afternoon rest. When she was made comfortable, I bent over her and said, "Mom, you get your rest. I will see you later."

Mom reached up and stroked my face with her frail, stiff, arthritic fingers and spoke, ever so plainly, like the first time I saw her, "Lee, I've been dreaming and hoping and praying that you would come, and you did. God answered my prayer. I love you my son."

With that she closed her eyes and drifted into a deep sleep. I just stood at the door and watched as she lay there, gently breathing in once again the fragrance of the honeysuckle that grew just outside her window. I took a few steps over to her bedside, lifted my hand and gently touched her cheek and said, "See you later, mom. I love you too. I'm so sorry I have waited so long to tell you."

I turned away from the bedside, expecting Nora to still be present in the room, but she had gone, evidently desiring to provide a time of privacy for my mother and me.

I glanced back at mom, just to make sure she was resting comfortably. Little was I aware that it would be the last time I would see my mother alive.

CHAPTER 12

The afternoon sun was warm but not really hot. I enjoyed the short trip out to the farm with the top down on my car. I think I drove slowly because I heard a meadowlark singing and wanted to hear its song. How long had it been since I had taken time to listen to that beautiful song? Our farm was always full of meadowlarks and sometimes even the two radical geese that stayed up by the house would tilt their long necks and heads as though they were also enjoying their songs.

In addition to the meadowlarks, the mockingbird's repertoire added to the music of the prairie land. What a blessed part of God's creation! And I never realized how much I had missed it. So I just parked the car for awhile and listened. No other cars were on the road.

Later, when I pulled up in front of the farm house, I saw Ron coming from around behind the house. "Hi Lee," he called out as he waved to me. "I heard a car coming so thought I would come around and see who it is."

"Hi Ron," I said. "I just thought I would come back out and ask if it was alright for me to hike down to the lake and look it over for awhile."

"Sure," he replied, "but why don't you drive to it?"

"Well, I was thinking whether I really wanted to drive my car over that dirt road."

"You don't have to drive your car," he said. "Take the pickup that is out by the shed. It's used to every bump on this farm and it needs to be driven today. I haven't driven it in quite awhile."

"Okay," I agreed, "However, I really could use the walk. It would be good for me. As I remember it's only about a quarter of a mile, isn't it?"

"Yes," he said, "or maybe just a little more than that, more like three quarters."

"On the other hand," I said, "if you don't mind I'll take the pickup. I'll probably not be gone very long. I just have some serious thinking to do and that is a good place to do it. Prior to the time I left home I would do most of my best thinking setting on the bank with my feet in the water."

"You, too?" he asked. "Every time I had to make a major decision – or even little ones for that matter, or I just wanted to get away to a place where I could get my head cleared up, I would hike down to the lake. It was always quiet, except for the birds singing and a little breeze rustling through the cattails. I love those meadowlarks and also the mockingbirds. Did you know they can mock about thirty other bird songs?"

He continued, obviously enjoying the remembering as much as I. "Once in awhile I would fish. I kept a pole and line under a tree by the lake and when I was in the mood I would put some worms on the hook and fish for perch.

"You know what? Every time I brought my 'catch' back up to the house, Gran would cook it, even if it were only one or two small fish, and she would say, 'Ron, that's a mighty fine catch of fish. We'll have them for dinner. That should be plenty for everyone.' Know what else? I noticed that she would always have some other kind of meat on the table. She always made me feel proud of my catch of fish."

"Yeah, Ron," I said, "I know what you mean. She did the same for me. She was like that, wasn't she?"

"The keys are in the pickup. Help yourself and stay as long as you like. I usually get supper ready around six and if you are still here you're welcome to stay and eat with me."

"I'll think about it," I said, as I started the pickup and put it in gear. The vehicle began to move across the open space between the house and barn, the dust rose easily from behind the back wheels and soon blotted out Ron's image that I saw as I was looking through the rearview mirror. He had one hand in the air, waving at me. With the other hand he held the crutch on which he was now leaning. I noticed that he had switched from using a cane to the crutch.

It is difficult to believe that a lake stays exactly the same for almost one quarter of a century. As I parked and exited the pickup I began to walk toward the lake. It seemed as though it was just like I remembered it when I used to come here as a kid with Old True. The ducks and geese were still floating around on the surface just a bit from the shore. They looked the same as they did back then. They even looked like the very same ducks. Of course, don't all ducks look alike?

They paid little attention to me and there was no old dog present to bark, jump in the water and encourage them to take flight. They simply, quietly and gently paddled more toward the center of the lake when they first took notice of my presence.

The water in the lake was crystal clear and, altogether, covered about ten acres. I had forgotten how clear it was. Most bodies of water in this part of the country are a muddy brown color, but this lake was always clear. My dad used to say it was the best lake in the state because it was about the only clear lake in the state.

Evidently it was fed by a spring that bubbled up in one part of the lake and overflowed into a small stream that ran down through the pasture and by the barn near the house. It provided excellent drinking water for the livestock. The stream took the water to them; they didn't have to walk all the way out here for it, therefore they never muddied it up by wading in it.

Cattails and rushes grew close to the lake's edge and sometimes ventured a few feet out into it. There were three small groves of shade trees back a ways from the water's edge, providing respite from the summer's heat to any animals, including the cows and horses. Mostly, however, they provided shade for fox, squirrels and an occasional coyote that happened to wander into the area. The trees are all grown up now.

I walked over to the edge of the lake and stood for a long time drinking in the beauty of the location. I bent down and put my hand in the water, feeling its coolness in the middle of a very warm afternoon sun. Here, in the middle of a flat and spacious prairie lay one of the most beautiful lakes that is rarely enjoyed by anyone. And it seemed to me that it had been waiting all this time just for me to come and enjoy it. And that I did!

"Do you remember when you used to bring Bonnie here for a walk and a swim?"

I jerked myself around to see if someone had followed me. No one! My submerged thoughts are once again coming to the surface, speaking loud and clear.

Yes, I thought, *I remember those special times when we would come out here all by ourselves, sometimes walking, sometimes racing each other, sometimes on horseback, sometimes holding hands, sometimes not, but always with a kind of unspoken, shared love — or at least a very deep liking, for each other. I preferred to think of it as love.*

I said out loud, "Of course I remember. How could I forget?"

But that is exactly what I had done. I had intentionally forgotten it by putting it out of my mind and I had done such a good job of it that I also wiped out all the special happy experiences we enjoyed together. I was afraid to admit that I loved her. When I tried to approach the subject with a couple of my friends and even my dad, I can remember them all saying the same thing, "Oh, you're both too young to be in love. You don't even know what love is all about. Wait 'til you grow up a little."

I think they were wrong. I think I was trying to show her my love when we were in the attic at the farm house. I just went about doing it the wrong way and wound up lusting rather than loving and hurting her and destroying what love she may have had for me. How I wish I could go back and start all over again. But that can't happen!

It's too late to think about that now. I have to figure out what to do about my job in Portland and, at the same time, how to handle things here at the farm.

I could just go back to Portland to my work and when Ron's twenty-fifth birthday comes in a few weeks, the farm, according to dad's revised will, will belong to him. That may not be a bad idea. I will give it some serious thought.

I like Ron. I only wish I had known him when he was little. I think he would be a good person to have control of the farm. After all, from all indications, it would still remain in the Edwards family.

"Is that what you really want to do?"

I didn't even bother to look around this time because I had come to realize that the two sides of my brain liked to talk with each other.

"No, that isn't really what I want to do, but it seems the sensible thing to do." I said, as I turned my head from right to left.

Right: *"Well, what do you want to do?"*

Left: "I don't know what I want to do. That's why I'm sitting here on the side of this lake trying to figure it out."

Right: *"Do you really like your job all that much?"*

Left: "Well it pays good. It has good benefits. I like my boss. I have a good home and a car."

Right: *"So?"*

Left: "So, what?"

Right: *"So is that all you want out of life, good salary, good benefits, a nice home and a car?"*

Left: "It's a good start. What's wrong with it."

Right: *"How about friends and family and relationships and roots and laughter and meadowlark song and wind in the trees and honeysuckle?"*

Left: "You mean that I should leave all that and come back here to smell honeysuckle?"

Right: *"You've thought about it, right?"*

Left: "Sure, I've thought about it lots of times since I arrived back here and especially today after I saw the improvement in mom and the look of sheer happiness in her eyes."

Right: *"So, it's not so hard, is it?"*

Left: "What's not so hard? I said, what's not so hard?"

Silence!

CHAPTER 13

Ron had walked up behind me while I was busy talking with myself and when he spoke to me I almost jumped into the lake.

"Hi, Lee. I'm sorry if I startled you. "I decided to walk out to see if everything is okay."

"Sure, Ron," I said, after getting control of myself, "Everything is okay. At least I think it is. I've been trying to make a major decision related to my work in Portland and the farm here in Pryor."

"When I walked up I thought I heard you talking with someone, but I didn't see anyone."

"I *was* talking to someone, Ron. Me. It seems lately that I talk to myself a lot. Actually, I probably spend more time arguing with myself rather than talking. Consequently I seem to accomplish little in the process."

"Ever talk to yourself, Ron?" I asked.

"Oh, quite often!"

"What kind of things do you talk about with yourself, Ron

"Well, lately I've said things like 'Ron, how are you going to handle things here on the farm now that Gramps is gone and Gran is confined to a nursing home? How are you going to continue taking care of the animals when your injuries are not getting any better and the people in town get tired of helping out because they have their own work to do?

"I ask, 'Ron, what's going to happen when you can't run the tractor to plow the ground or plant the seed or harvest the corn? What are you going to do when you start getting old and there is no one to stand beside you to encourage you or share your life with you because they don't want to marry a cripple?'

"I ask myself, 'Ron, what's going to happen to the Edward's farm when you get old and you have no son to whom you can leave it like it has been passed from generation to generation of Edwards?'

"Oh yes, Lee, I talk to myself almost every day with those kinds of questions."

Ron was standing within arm's reach and I could look into those dark eyes and see the hurt, the frustration, the fear, the anger and all the other emotions that go with a sense of hopelessness. I could see a young man that had every right to have those feelings storm to the surface.

His eyes burned into mine and suddenly I knew what I had to do.

"Ron, I know that you already know what I'm going to say. At least I think you do, but I want to say it and I want to hear myself say it and admit the truth of it.

"A long time ago your mother and I......Ron, there was a time when your mother and I liked each other very much. In fact we loved each other. Ron, I....I believe I am your father. No, I know I am your father. I have no doubts about it. I am not sorry that I am your father. I am only sorry that it took me so long to admit to myself the truth of it."

It all came flooding to the surface and I couldn't quit. "I am so sorry that I failed you as a father and that you had to experience all the things you had to go through because I wasn't there for you from the beginning. I was too big of a coward and too self-centered to own up to my responsibility for what I did with your mother and in the process destroyed a beautiful love we had for each other."

"You have every right to hate me. I cannot blame you if you do. There is no way I can undo what has been done. All I can ask of you is that if you have it in your heart can you, will you, forgive me?"

Those dark eyes never moved or blinked for what seemed like an eternity. I could not tell if he was stunned by the news and was in a state of emotional shock or if what I said simply confirmed something of which he was already aware.

Without blinking, he said "I know. I think I have known that you were my dad ever since Gramps and Gran brought me to live with them when my step-dad told my mom he didn't want me in their house any more. I was only about four or five, but when mom brought me to talk with Gramps and Gran about me living with them permanently they were happy to do so. I began to wonder even then why, at their age, they would do that. Why would they want to raise a little kid when their own son was an adult and gone? And why would my mom so willingly leave me with them?

"Later, when I was a little older and began asking them questions, Gramps never said a lot. He just patted me on the shoulder, looked kind of sad and said, "When you get older." But when I talked with Gran she would have a certain look and smile and say, "Ronnie, you're just like my very own grandson."

"One time when I was about ten I asked her, 'Am I your real grandson?'"

Without hesitation, she said, "Yes, Ronnie – that's what she called me most of the time, Ronnie. Yes, Ronnie, you are my real grandson."

I asked, "Does that mean that your son, Lee, that ran away is my real dad?"

"Yes, Ronnie, our son that ran away is your real dad." Then she told me that they had known about it ever since they heard that my mom was pregnant with me. The two of you could hide very little from them or from people in town or from the ones at school. It seemed like everyone knew it but you.

"Lee, is that why my mom was sent away? Is that why you ran away and no one heard from you all this time?" His eyes reflected a mixture of anger, grief and loneliness.

"Ron, I don't think I was running away from them so much as I was trying to run away from me. I hated myself for what I did to your mother, but inside, I had to find some other reason for leaving so that I could live with myself. I told my folks I didn't want to be a farmer or live in a small town, but that I wanted to see the world and find myself. That never happened. I got just as far as Portland, Maine and I'm not sure that I ever found myself."

"Lee, it sounds strange to call you dad, so could I just call you Lee?"

"Sure, Ron. You can call me Lee."

"Lee, except for a few of your high school pictures that Gran had, I never knew what you looked like. Just the same, I hated you for a lot of years. I stood in front of your high school picture and told you that I hated you for what you did to my mom and then leave her to fend for herself in this small town.

"But Gran helped me to understand that if it hadn't happened I would not be here and they wouldn't have a grandson to love. That helped to take away some of the hatred I had for you, but not all of it.

"I went back to your picture and told you that I hated you also for leaving and making my mom have to marry someone else just because she thought I needed to have a father. Then when he said he didn't want me it crushed her when she realized she was married and I still didn't have a father.

"I hated you for those times I was in school and everyone else's dad came to the school events and mine didn't. I was always grateful to Gramps and Gran for making every effort to support me in my school activities, but I still missed having a dad like most of the other kids. Kids kept asking me about my dad and where he was. I didn't know, so I just said, 'he ran away.'

"I hated you for what you did to Gramps and Gran. You ran off and left them when they really needed you. They needed you, not just to work the farm or do the chores or carry on the Edward's name in the community, though that would have been a decent thing for you to do. They needed you because you were their son and they loved you, no matter how you acted or what you did. You really wounded them!

"They told me how you used to slide down the banister of the front stairs, in spite of them telling you not to do it. And how you did it when you were eighteen years old right in front of your dad, just to show him you could do it and dared him to discipline you.

"I used to do that same thing until Grandpa caught me, and one time was all it took. I can still feel the whipping I got.

"I hated you for treating them like dirt and walking all over their love for you.

"I hated you so much, that was all I could talk about for awhile. I got sick of hating you. Then one day, Gran sat down with me on the back porch and handed me a glass of iced tea. We drank our tea for a little while and she then said, "Ronnie," she still called me Ronnie and I was about fifteen or sixteen by then. 'Ronnie, you're going to have to get rid of that bitterness in your heart. It will kill you and then I will have lost not only my son, but also my grandson."

"What do you mean, Gran?" I asked her.

"Well every time you talk about your dad you speak nothing but words of hate for him. That hatred grows out of the bitterness in your heart. I can see the rage and anger rise up inside you and that you would like to physically beat him up and yell obscenities at him.

"Ronnie, you cannot continue to set around thinking up ways to get back at him. It won't do him any harm, because he doesn't even know about it, but it will kill you. You may never see him and do you want this unseen and unknown man to control your life and be responsible for whatever wrong thing may happen to you?"

"Gran had a way of saying things that cut to the chase. I began to think about what she said and decided I didn't want you to control my life and me not even knowing you."

"One day she came and sat down beside me on the front steps and said, 'Ronnie, have you forgiven your dad?'"

"Forgiven him?" I asked.

"Yes, forgiven him."

"Gran, what he did was wrong and what he is doing to you and Gramps is wrong and what he did to my mom and to me is wrong. Do you expect me to forgive him?"

"Yes. If you don't, your un-forgiveness will kill you."

"That seemed to always be her final shot, 'It'll kill you if you don't do it. Or, it'll kill you if you do that. Sometimes I felt like she might kill me if I didn't."

"You know? It almost did. That day when Gramps and I were taking food and seed out to the MacArthur place because all of them were sick and we were hit by that drunk driver and Gramps was killed and I was almost killed, part of it was because I was ranting and raving at Gramps about you and why you ran off and didn't stay at the farm to help them out.

"I have lived these past five years blaming myself for being responsible for Gramps' death, and blaming you because I felt responsible. I was distracting Gramps from his driving with my griping and complaining about you. He was looking over at me and telling me that I needed to forgive you or it would kill me. I think Gran had some influence on him.

"Anyhow, my un-forgiveness of you did play a part in killing him. I think he would have been aware of the drunk driver getting ready to run the stop sign on his side of the road if he hadn't been looking at me and trying to deal with my anger instead. Sometimes I wish it had been my side of the truck that was hit. Maybe then I would have been killed and Gramps would still be alive."

Ron looked at me for a moment with tears in his eyes, turned around, walked over to the pickup, got in it, turned on the ignition and drove off toward the house. He left me standing by the lake. All I could do was watch the pickup disappear in a cloud of dust.

I drove out to the lake from the house and he walked. He drove back to the house and I walked. It just happened. I don't think it was planned that way.

CHAPTER 14

"Is that you Ron? This is Susan at Mary-Martha nursing home. I think you will want to come in right away. Please come as soon as possible, it's important."

As I walked from the lake up to the house Ron was just getting into his pickup, preparing to leave. I called out to him to ask where he was going. He said that he had received a phone call from Susan at Mary-Martha and that he should come as soon as possible.

"What's happening?" I asked.

"I don't know; only that I should come," he yelled as he pulled away in the pickup.

"I'll follow you in my car." By the time I had finished saying that he was already headed down the lane to the highway.

We arrived at about the same time and walked into the front doors together, but no words were spoken as we moved directly to the nurses' station near room 120.

"I'm glad you came quickly, Ron - and Mr. Edwards. There has been a dramatic change in your grandmother's condition. Shortly after the lunch time today and the excitement for her at that time, she was helped to get into her bed for rest. She normally takes her nap following lunch.

"We check on our residents fairly regularly – every half hour or so, when they are taking their naps. Each time we looked in on your grandmother, she appeared to be resting very comfortably, breathing easily and with a peaceful countenance about her. She looked like she was resting really well.

"When we noticed that she was napping longer than usual we went in to make sure she was alright and to wake her up for her afternoon tea and snack. It was then that we discovered that she was not sleeping but had passed away sometime in her sleep. That is when we immediately tried to call you at the farm, but there was no answer until just awhile ago when I got hold of you, Ron. Thank you for coming."

It was easy to take note of the fact that the nurse directed her conversation to Ron about his grandmother. At first I felt a little left out or maybe a little offended, but then I realized that Ron had been the one there for the folks through these last twenty or so years. He was the one who helped mom with the arrangements for dad's funeral. He was the one who had to take the responsibility for checking mom in to Mary-Martha. He was the one who made sure the bills were paid. He was the one who knew the staff and they knew him.

I was the stranger in the place with little or no knowledge of all that had been happening. It was only natural that he should be the one to whom they were directing their conversation. But for some reason, it still caused a little anger and jealousy to rise to the surface. After all, I was their son and he was their grandson.

The nurse asked us to follow her in to mom's room. It did not feel the same as it did when I left it a few hours earlier, when I spoke to mom as she lay down to rest. "See you later, mom." I did not realize at the time that would be the last words I would speak to her.

As I stood there looking at the lifeless body of the one who had birthed me into this world, I could not help but grieve over the many lost opportunities that she had offered me to experience the kind of peace she had throughout her life, regardless of the circumstances.

When I was going through some tough time as a high school student, wondering how I was going to pass a test or make the team or find a date, she would simply say, "Lee, you just have to have faith. It will work out okay, you'll see." And then she would smile, give me a little hug, which I always seemed to resist, and go on her way humming some kind of tune. She had such peace in her life. How did she do it? That was twenty-five years ago and she still has it. You can see it in her face, even as she lies dead on that bed.

I looked at Ron. He had knelt beside the bed and was holding mom's hands and gently caressing her arm and speaking something very softly to her. His voice was very broken and tear-filled. Finally he just lay his head over on her arm and began to cry unashamedly. He had lost the second person in his life that meant more to him than life itself.

I really wanted to reach out and place my hand on his shoulder to let him know that I was there; that I shared in his grief and understood how he felt. But I didn't because I hadn't and I didn't. I didn't understand his grief because I had not experienced the close knit and loving kind of relationship that he and my parents had experienced and I truly didn't know how he felt.

I realized that it is an empty phrase when people say, 'I know how you feel,' when they really don't because they haven't gone through the exact same experience or had the same kind of shared relationship.

So I just stood there with folded hands hanging in front of me and the memory of one short week with a mother who was glad that I had come back and with whom I had experienced just over half a day watching her do physical therapy and making every effort to show me how happy she was that I was there.

Tears began to well up in my eyes, some from sorrow, others from envy, as I looked at Ron kneeling and grieving for mom and mom resting from her labors without me ever really coming to know her like he did and wishing I could. It was too late.

I felt a hand on my shoulder. "Mr. Edwards?" I turned to look into the face of Nurse Nora. "Mr. Edwards, Lee, I am so sorry about your mother. She was a very special woman and all of us loved to take care of her because she was always so easy to care for. She made every effort to help, even though her thinking and her muscular coordination would not work together. We will all miss her. I just want you to know that we are sorry for your loss."

"Thank you, Nora," I said. "I do appreciate your kindness and the obviously good care that you gave to mom. I only wish I had known her. Twenty five years is a long time to be away. In this case, it's a whole lifetime!"

CHAPTER 15

The service was planned to be held at the Trinity Community Church of Pryor with the Rev. Robert Reinfeld delivering the Eulogy. Ron did most of the planning of the service with the pastor. He was the right one to do it because he knew her and he knew the pastor. I was there, but interjected a comment only when they asked me what I thought. Since I knew nothing about how a funeral was to be conducted I simply agreed with what was suggested.

The service was set for Sunday afternoon at 3:00 o'clock with refreshments served in the social hall following the service. The women of the church were glad to be able to serve in this way to show their love for one of their own. The sanctuary was packed with mom's friends and acquaintances. It looked like all of Pryor was there.

Ron and I were the only two left in the Edwards family. Everyone was reminded of this when the obituary was read and that Melissa Edwards was preceded in death by all the previous Edwards and Perkins [mom's maiden name] family members, except for her son, Lee, and grandson, Ron.

Therefore, when it came time for the service, we sat together near the front, each grieving in our own way. I don't remember much of the service or even what a service was supposed to be like, except for what was discussed in Rev. Reinfeld's office.

I had been away from the church for over twenty-five years. That was part of the decision I made when I left Pryor, to leave behind all the things that remind me of the small town, including church. Prior to leaving Pryor, I left the church.

Nevertheless, as I sat there beside Ron in a place in which he was obviously comfortable and surrounded by many people who held him and my parents in high regard and respect, I could not help but feel the warmth and peace that was present. Even though it was my mom's funeral and I could sense lots of peoples' eyes regularly glancing at me, I didn't seem to feel distraught. Her words came back to me from years ago, "Lee you just have to have faith. It will be okay."

The Reverend Reinfeld spoke for awhile following some piano music and a solo by one of the ladies in the church. I don't remember much of what he said, only that mom was loved by everyone in the community. He spoke of how she and dad had helped so many and how they had raised Ron and how glad she was to see Lee when he came to visit a few days ago and some other things like that.

In the midst of it I was thinking 'what you are saying is really nice, but she's gone. She's gone and now I will never be able to tell her or show her or make up for all the lost years that were lost because of my wrong decisions and bad judgments. She's gone!'

About the time I was thinking that "she's gone," the Reverend said, "Now I want to conclude my remarks by quoting a poem that I used at CJ's funeral about five years ago. Ron asked me if I would use it today. It is called, 'They Walk Softly," by Robert Kerr." I listened.

"They are not gone who pass beyond the clasp of hands,

out from the strong embrace.

They are but come so close we need not look to see,

or try to catch the sound of feet.

I didn't hear much of the rest of the poem, except occasional parts, because the first words made me realize that I had forfeited the clasp of her hands and the strong embraces from which I pushed myself away as a teenager. I felt only the gentle touch of her gnarled fingers on my face as I prepared to leave her in the nursing home. I did hear the closing line of the poem and inwardly knew that was true for mom.

*They are not lost who find the light of sun and stars and God."**

Following a few more comments by the Reverend the service ended with some somber organ music by a Mrs. Orrin Webb and with the men from the funeral home opening the casket. I would really have preferred to keep it closed, but the Reverend and Ron thought it would help the people have closure. So, it was opened and everyone began to file by, pausing for a moment and some final word.

When all had exited the sanctuary, Ron and I were left alone with mother and grandmother lying in the open casket. I held back a little to let Ron say his goodbyes. It was a very difficult and tearful time for him. When he stepped away I moved up closer to take a last look at the woman who had given me birth and with whom I had shared life – such as it was, for eighteen years and one week - eighteen years before I left Pryor and one week after I returned, prior to her death.

In many ways it was like saying goodbye to a stranger since I had not been with her or made contact with her for twenty five years. I think I grieved some there by the casket, but not so much over her death as for all the lost years that I could have enjoyed her life.

As I turned to leave her there, I simply spoke, "See you later, mom."

"Will you see her later?"

Looking around, and seeing no one, I quickly left the sanctuary and joined everyone else who was gathered in the social hall for refreshments. I did not feel like refreshments or hearing people tell me how much my folks missed me or how great they were to Ron or how great he was to them. I felt like an outsider.

These people seem to have the kind of faith that mom evidently tried to instill in me all those years ago. Perhaps I can know it someday, but right now I didn't want to hear any more condolences or forced sympathetic remarks. I knew many of them knew that I was the Edwards' prodigal, runaway son.

As I turned to leave I once again ran in to Nurse Nora. I bumped her arm and caused her to spill some of her punch. After apologizing profusely and endeavoring to help her clean up the spill and wipe the cake frosting off her arm, I quipped, "So, we meet again."

She said, "Mr. Edwards, Lee, you're hazardous!"

We both chuckled, and loudly enough that it broke the solemnity of the gathering. Others gathered around to help Nora get her blouse cleaned up. I felt embarrassed with all the attention that I had drawn to her and to me.

I apologized to Nora once again and following a few polite handshakes and unthinking comments like "Gotta go! See you later," I found a way to quickly exit the building, get in my car and drive back to the motel for a time of quiet grief all by myself.

And to decide what to do next!

"Will you?"

"Will I? Will I what?

"Will you see her later, like you said?"

"Who? Nora?"

"No, your mom! You said "See you later, mom"

"When did I say that?"

"You said it when you walked away from her casket just awhile ago. Will you?'"

"Well, people say that all the time even when they know they probably won't ever see that person again. It's just a way of saying goodbye. You don't really mean it, especially when...when you're standing at a casket."

"Why not, especially when you're standing at a casket? It's possible, you know."

"Oh, for heaven's sake, I don't want to get involved in this religious and churchy stuff about life after death if that's what you're talking about. I've had enough of that already today.

"However, I wouldn't mind seeing Nora again later."

CHAPTER 16

I lay on the motel bed and stared at the ceiling.

Was there anything keeping me in Pryor? That nightmare? Was mom 'treading my dream-led paths of sleep,' like the Reverend said? The purpose of that so-called dream I had that brought me here was, to my way of thinking, met. Mom had been praying that I would come, and I did, she saw me again before she died and she died happy.

Whatever it was that I was to learn at the house evidently happened. That place reminded me of what Bonnie and I had done, plus all the other things that I had buried in my subconscious for all these years. It reminded me of how much of a disappointment I had been to everyone, but mostly to myself.

But, truthfully, was it worth all the effort to come here just to find out how worthless I am or what I have missed out on all these years?

Laying there on the bed with my hands cupped behind my head I continued to stare at the ceiling, from behind tired, drooping, moist eyelids. Thank goodness, it is finished!

"Is it?"

My eyes popped open as I sat up on my elbows, "Who's...?'

Right: *"Right! I asked, is it worth it and is it finished?"*

"Worth what?"

Right: *"Were the things you have discovered about yourself worth the trip back to Pryor?"*

"It seems a long way to travel just to find out things that I already knew."

Right: *"Well, you may have known them, but you had long since forgotten that you knew them because you didn't want to deal with them. Right? Right!"*

"Perhaps. I'll just have to think about it."

Actually, I really didn't have to think about it at all. I came back, found out about my parents, visited the farm home, met my now grown son, Ron, who was born to my high school girlfriend, and helped to attend to the burial of my mother. That's a plate full for less than a week.

The only remaining thing yet to do is to let the farm go to Ron on his twenty-fifth birthday in a couple of weeks, then I have nothing left for which to stay here. I don't even have to sign any papers because it is already written into my folk's will. The farm can be Ron's and I can go back to Portland and my work. A reasonable solution!

With that solution firmly in mind, I drifted off to a fitful sleep.

The jangling of the motel room phone brought me back from sleep as I still lay on the bed with the same clothes I had on when I attended the funeral. The room was dark. Looking at the bedside clock with it luminous red dials I saw that it was 11:30 p.m. It was an unwelcome call.

"What do you mean I won't have a job if I'm not there by tomorrow morning? You said that I could have a week and my job would be waiting for me. Look, I need that job and we agreed that I could come here and take care of some family matters. My mother died and we just had her funeral this afternoon. Doesn't that count for anything? How can I possibly get all the way back to Portland in time to be at work tomorrow morning?

"Do you know what time it is?... What?... You know there is no way in...on earth I can get back to Portland and in to the office by 7:30 in the morning to prepare for a court appearance.

"What?... You don't really mean that! ... Well, then you can just take your job and shove...Hello!"

I slammed the receiver back on the cradle as the anger came rocketing to the surface. I was on my feet, stomping around the room and muttering obscenities that I had long since forgotten were stored in my vocabulary bank.

I need that blinkety-blank job and that blinkety-blank so and so promised me it would be waiting for me. Couldn't he understand and have a little sympathy for the situation in which I find myself? He jolly well better have some kind of severance package ready for me or I'll sue the pants off him and that miserable company.

"Now what do I do?" I asked myself.

"Do you really need that job?"

The Brain thing doesn't even faze me anymore. I find myself doing it quite often for some reason. Perhaps it's because there's no one else around here to talk with about what's going on so I talk with myself.

"Of course I need that job. I'm forty three years old and I could have kept that job and have a good retirement and all the other perks that go with it. Of course I need that job."

"Well, you don't have it, and now that you don't have it what will you do?"

"If I knew what I was going to do I wouldn't have to ask myself that question, would I? Right?"

"Why don't you give it some thought? Think about it. You are now without a job in Portland. You do have a condo in Portland with no mortgage payments. You have a good savings account in Portland that you have built up in the fifteen years you have had the job. You have made some risky investments but they have earned you considerable income. You have a car. Is there anything besides your condo and bank account that ties you to Portland?"

I mused, "That has been my home for almost twenty years. I have a lot of frien…. Well, come to think of it I can't name any really close friends because I've been too busy with my work and didn't have time. All my relationships with women have been disastrous, so I certainly have no reason to go back for that.

"Maybe I should just say that Portland is a place where I have lived all those years, but it never became home to me. It was a place to live and work and… what? Run away to?"

"Then why are you considering going back?"

"For one thing, I have a severance paycheck coming and I'm going to collect it! If they're going to fire me then they're going to make it worth my while."

CHAPTER 17

"I don't know, Ron. He checked out early this morning, put his stuff in his car and pulled out."

Lee was not at the motel.

"I don't know, Ron. He stopped by last night following your grandmother's funeral, picked up a few items and put gas in his car. I haven't seen him since. He didn't have much to say."

Lee was not at Ben's.

"Where could he have gone?" Ron thought. *"He didn't stop by the farm or phone me. I saw him leave the reception early but didn't have opportunity to ask him what he was going to do. I needed to talk over some things about the farm before he disappeared again.*

"Lee, where are you?"

Ron's next stop was to see Nora at the nursing home.

"No Ron. He didn't stop by here. What made you think he would?"

"Well," Ron said, "you talked with him quite a bit when he came out to see Gran and I saw the two of you talking and laughing in the church fellowship hall following the funeral so I just thought maybe he might have stopped by to thank you or to say goodbye or something."

"No," said Nora, "he didn't stop by and I haven't seen him since yesterday. He's probably around town somewhere. I'm sure he'll show up. I wouldn't worry about it if I were you."

"I am worried about it because I need to talk with him about something."

CHAPTER 18

As I drove down the freeway I talked to myself.   *"It's going to be a very long drive back from Pryor to Portland. It's over fourteen hundred miles. That's going to take me almost two full days. There was no way I could have made it before today. The funeral wasn't until yesterday afternoon. What do they expect of me?"*

Well, anyway the sun is warm, the top is down and I might just as well take my time and enjoy the trip. No job to return to and so, like the commercial says, 'I'm free to fly about the country."

That's what I'll do. I'll just take my sweet time, but when I get there they'd better get ready to hear me out. In the meantime I might as well listen to some travelling music.

Oh, John Denver! Just great! Where did that CD come from? I'm not sure I even like Denver's music. It's a little too nostalgic for my blood, but at least it carries some kind of story with it. "Country Road, take me home, to the place where I belong.....

"Where do you belong, Lee?"

"Well, certainly not West Virginia." I laughingly said, "I've never been there and don't plan on going there."

"Where do you belong, and plan on going, Lee?"

"Okay brain. Have it your way. There are only two places left, Portland or Pryor and my home is in Portland."

"Is it? You have a condo there but is that your home?"

"Look, if this is some psychological mind game it's got to quit. 'Lee, quit talking to yourself.'"

I pulled over into the closest Rest Area. I didn't need to go to the restroom, but I did need to get off the highway before I became a danger to myself and everyone else on the road. I pulled into a parking space away from the main building and in the shade of a large oak tree.

"Man," I said, as I laid my head on the steering wheel. "I've just got to quit talking to myself."

"Lee, you're not talking to yourself. And it isn't your right brain and left brain talking to you either. You're not even close."

I hit myself up 'side the head at the same time I said, "Then what the heck is going on?"

"Lee, do you remember when you first came back to Pryor? You came in response to a dream- or nightmare, and at the time you said that you felt like something was crying out from within your soul and spirit for you to return to the place of your birth?"

"Vaguely," I responded. "I guess I could have said it. I don't remember."

"Well, you did and you were right in thinking that. Lee, I am you. I am your heart, crying out within you, trying to help you tie together all the dangling loose ends of your life. You have always been a person that operates almost totally on your will and emotions, your soul. You have a strong will. You've always had a strong will, even when you were a kid. Right?"

"Well, mom always seemed to say something like that," I replied.

"I'm trying to help you put a little thought into following your spirit, your heart.. You think of me as right brain left brain, but I am far more than that. I am what makes you, you."

"As your spirit I am the one that makes you glad to hear the meadowlark song or enjoy the smell of the honeysuckle. I am that part of you that makes you see the clear water in the lake and appreciate the way the ducks glides effortlessly on its surface.

"I am that part of you that makes you like to hug a mangy old dog or chase cantankerous geese or catch a perch. I am the one that causes you to enjoy the warm sun or smile at a stranger walking out of a convenience store.

"Lee, I am that part of you that helps you remember the wisdom of your mother or look forward to riding in the pickup with your father when he's sober.

"I am that part of you that tried to get you to understand the importance of believing in yourself and the importance of forgiveness.

"Lee, you were too busy running away to believe that anyone could still care for you. You have listened to your own will and emotions for so long you have failed to remember those times when I have tried to help you discover that part of yourself that really matters – your heart.

"I am that part of you that tried to help you understand that others love you and see you as someone special, even when you were too afraid or too angry to accept it for yourself.

"I am the one that quickened your heart to love a young girl and the one who is able to help you have the ability to love again.

"Now, Lee, think! Where is your heart leading you? Not your will or you rational mind, but your heart? Follow your heart! It's time for you to get with it and follow your heart!"

Larry Eddings

"Follow my heart? Where does my heart want to go? Where is it going? Where do *I* want to go? Geez! Help me!"

"Okay, they can mail the damn severance check."

The next overpass was only about five more miles down the road and by the time I arrived there I knew what I was going to do – follow my heart - a whole new concept to me.

I exited, went back over the freeway and took the merge lane, heading back toward Pryor. About that time Denver hit the chorus, "Country Road, take me home to the place I was born." No, those weren't the right words in the song, but that's what I heard in my heart. And this wasn't a country road, it was a freeway, but it accomplished the same purpose. It's heading me home. Home! That suddenly had a good ring to it. New, but good!

"Oops! Need to watch out for those eighteen wheelers," I said out loud. "It could kill you." Where have I heard that line before?

"There, that wasn't so hard, was it?"

"No," I said. "It wasn't all that hard."

The miles back to Pryor seemed like an eternity. It's so strange that when you don't want to get somewhere, the time goes by extra fast, but when you're in a hurry to get there, every hour seems like two. By this time it was nearing sunset. Finally,

PRYOR, CITY LIMITS

A City for all Seasons

Population, 6500

124

"Counting pets and farm animals, I'll bet."

Where to? Back to the motel or out to the farm? First I had better stop and get some gas before I go anywhere.

"Hi Ben," I said as I stepped through the front door of his convenience store.

"Oh, hi Lee," he said. We were wondering what happened to you. Ron has been asking around town if anyone had seen you today."

"Well," I replied, "to be truthful, I was headed back to Portland. My boss called late last night to tell me that unless I could be there by 7:30 this morning I was fired. No way to make it, so, I'm fired. I was going back to get my severance check, but on the way I changed my mind."

"I was wondering why you checked out and left town so early this morning without saying anything to anyone," Ben said.

But I think I knew what he was thinking, so I said it for him, "Kind of reminiscent of the old days when I was about eighteen, checking out and not letting anyone know where I went, huh?"

Before he could respond, I remarked, "Well, now that I've changed my mind and decided to come back here to Pryor, I guess I will have to figure out what to do with my stuff in Portland and also what to do about Ron and the farm."

"Well, Lee," said Ben, "there's a little more to it than that."

"But Ben," I reminded him, "you said that Ron would be twenty-five in a few weeks and when he is the farm will automatically go to him according my folk's will. Will that make any difference now that I am back in the picture and maybe plan to stay here?"

"No." Ben replied, "Not unless you decide to make an issue of it and contest the will. You have a right to since you are their only son and heir."

"I don't want to contest it. The farm rightfully belongs to Ron. He worked for my folks since he was a little kid. That farm is home to him and to take it away from him would not be the right thing to do. I want him to have it.

"I have enough financial resources to take care of myself for awhile. However, maybe he will let me live on the place with him until I can get established here in town."

"That's a mighty decent thing for you to do, Lee. Of course, the farm isn't as big as it used to be, since your dad sold off some of the land and bought the Feed and Seed Store. And it's a little run down from what it used to be. But it's still plenty big for Ron to take care of, considering his physical condition."

"However," continued Ben, "there's more to think about than the farm. Your folks also owned that Feed and Seed Store that I just was telling you about."

"What about it?" I asked.

"Well, when the store began to be profitable for your dad he took on a young fellow to help him. You may remember him, Clint Burdett? I think he was a year ahead of you in school. He played on the football team.

"Yeah," I said, "I remember him alright. Always the hero, homecoming king, top of his class, voted most likely to succeed and all that. I do remember him."

Ben continued, "When he graduated he went off to a community college somewhere and got an Associate Degree in Business Administration. When he came back your dad hired him on to help run the store so that he could concentrate on farming."

"Sounds like dad made a good decision there," I said.

'It was a good decision, for awhile anyway," Ben said. "The store had been profitable when your dad ran it. However, after a few years, things changed. People still traded at the store, bought their seeds and other supplies there, but there never seemed to be enough profit to pay the bills. CJ confided in me that it kept coming up short each month."

"In the meantime Clint bought himself a big four wheel SUV, one of those things with a Hemi engine. You know, the kind that young people seem to like to drive now. He roared around town like he was still high school homecoming king and he was in his late thirties.

"When your folks began to question Clint about how the business was doing and said they wanted to see the books he got steamed and asked if they were accusing him of mismanaging the business. They simply said they wanted to see the books and have me audit them like they always do in order to see why the business was not doing well.

"Old Charlie Higgins and I had audited their books for years before Clint took over, and even for a few years after he did, and it was a natural thing for your folks to say to him."

I asked, "Why did Clint get so steamed over getting the books audited? That's something a business does on an annual basis. It should have been no surprise to him."

"Well," continued Ben, "I guess since he had a Business Administration degree he felt he could take care of the books himself and didn't need some local yokels making a mess of them. Seems he already had made a mess of them and didn't want anyone to know about it.

"I guess he knew what we would find out if we audited, so he just up and disappeared one night. His family said they didn't know where he had gone and they thought it was a terrible thing for the Edwards to accuse their boy of stealing from them. After all, he had tried to help Ben out for years so that he could spend time running the farm. Now the Burdett name had been maligned all over the county because of their accusations.

"Anyhow, we audited the books and found a very big discrepancy of some fifteen thousand dollars for just the past year. He had worked the books to make it look like the receipts and expenditures balanced with a small profit left over, but it didn't take long to find out otherwise. He had been dipping in the till on a regular basis."

"What did the folks do?" I asked.

"As much as they hated the idea they talked with me about taking Clint to court in an effort to recover some of their losses. We were preparing to do just that when your dad was killed in that accident.

Ben paused for a short time while scratching the side of his head. "And that's another thing, Lee," he said, "about the accident."

"What about the accident?" I asked.

"Well, at first we all thought - because we were told by the Sheriff, that it was probably some drunken guy who had had a fight with his wife and ran the stop sign, hit your dad's pickup, saw what had happened, got scared and high-tailed it. It was a hit and run accident.

"When Sheriff Burdett checked the scene he told us that that was probably what happened. However, others of us who went out to the scene could see that there were long tracks in the side gravel road like someone had really stepped on the gas to get their rig moving fast. And then there were tread burn marks on the highway where they had obviously backed up after the impact and sped away, burning rubber both ways on the blacktop.

"Another interesting thing about the accident is that the impact was level with your dad's head, not down were a normal bumper would hit in the middle of the door. It was like the bumper was on a higher rig."

"Wasn't the accident investigated by the Sheriff or the Highway Patrol?" I asked.

"Oh, yes," said Ben, "But for some reason they could never find the hit and run driver or the rig that caused the accident. However, we all had our suspicions and told the Sheriff so. He was really riled over what we told him."

"Did you say that the Sheriff's name is Burdett?" I asked. "Is he some relative of Clint?"

"As a matter of fact, he is," said Ben. "He is Jerry Burdett, Clint's uncle."

"And nothing has ever been settled regarding the accident?" I asked.

"No," said Ben, "Your mom and Ron have been making effort to find out who did it, but were stymied at every turn by Sheriff Burdett who kept insisting that your dad was killed by a drunken driver and they would track him down in due time, so just let it rest.

"Nevertheless, your mom wouldn't let it rest and kept on the Sheriff for about three years with no help from him or his department. I think that played a major part in her having a stroke. She was totally frustrated by the lack of effort to find out who did it.

"Most of us think that no effort at all was made to find out who did it. We have no way of proving it, but several of us in town believe that Clint was so angry over being discovered that he deliberately drove his SUV into the side of your dad's pickup and that's what killed him. However, we have no proof, just suspicions.

"Burdett is not the Sheriff any longer. We voted him out of office the next time around. Like Clint, he also left town and no one knows where he is.

"I'm sorry to have to tell you all of this but it all has to do with the fact that the Feed and Seed Store, such as it is with all its back taxes, still belongs to the Edward's estate. You will have to make a decision what to do with it. Ron's not in a physical or mental state right now to handle both the farm and the store.

"Ben, just what is Ron's physical and mental condition? I know he was in the wreck, but that was five years ago and I notice he is still limping and using a cane, and sometimes, a crutch. Has he tried surgery to repair his hip or leg or whatever else was injured?"

"It's his hip," said Ben. When the car was hit on your dad's side it threw Ron into the door on his side and broke his right hip. No, actually it shattered his right hip. Doctors tried to piece it back together as best they could. They used steel plates and bolts, but they said it would never work like it should."

"I suppose I should be asking Ron these questions, but, Ben, has he ever considered hip replacement? I know a couple of people in Portland who have had total hip replacements and they have worked really well; they walk like they never had a surgery."

"Oh, Ron has considered that quite a bit, and so have the rest of us who want to help him, but have you thought about the cost involved? It is way beyond the means of any of us here in town and Ron has no insurance to cover it.

"Insurance from the accident barely covered the cost of replacing the old pickup and some of the hospital expenses. Ron has resigned himself to limping for the rest of his life and has tried to make adjustments accordingly. He does really well for the shape he's in."

"I can vouch for that," I said. "The other day he walked the half mile or so from the farm house to the lake. I had driven there in the pickup and here he comes walking up later to make sure I was okay. He drove the pickup back and I walked."

I didn't feel a need to tell Ben why he drove the pickup and I walked. I didn't think it was necessary.

I checked back in at the motel until I had opportunity to talk with Ron about staying at the farm.

.

CHAPTER 19

"Mr. Edwards, welcome back," said the fellow at the desk. "You received a call early this morning after you checked out. I didn't know how to get hold of you, so I took the number and told her that if I saw you I would get the message to you. Here's the number and her name. I think she said that she's a mortgage lady."

I checked back in to the room I had previously occupied and made the call. Marie was indeed a mortgage lady. She is the one who helped me buy the Portland condo in the first place.

"Marie, this is Lee Edwards. You called early this morning, but I was out of town at the time. What's up?"

"Mr. Edwards, I have a couple who is interested in buying your condo here in Portland."

"The condo?" I asked.

"Yes," she said, "that is if you are interested in selling it. They really like it. Have you thought of selling it?

"Yes," I answered, "as a matter of fact I have been considering selling it."

I didn't tell her that I had been considering it only within the last few minutes since she had mentioned it.

"So, someone is interested in buying it?" I asked, repeating the very thing she had just told me

"Yes," she said, " and they would like to do so as soon as possible."

"As soon as possible?" I asked, continuing to repeat the very thing I had heard from her.

"Yes," she replied, "and they want to know how soon they might be able to occupy it if you're willing to sell?" And, are you willing to sell the furniture with the condo?

"They want to occupy it soon and also buy the furniture?" I repeated, once again. "Well, I think that can be arranged."

As Marie continued to give the details related to the possible sale of the condo my mind was in overdrive. I glanced up at the ceiling and asked myself "How much better could it get?"

"Indeed! How much better can it get?"

The conversation with Marie went on for quite awhile as we talked about price, which was almost one hundred percent capital gain over what I had paid for it fifteen years ago. Then we talked of occupation, mortgage agreements, signing papers and all the other things that go with the buying and selling of properties.

She said she would take care of all the details and fax me the papers if I would get her a fax number to which she could send them.

The conversation ended with Marie a very happy woman – she could see the commission on that size of a sale, and with a very happy Lee – I didn't have to worry about what I would be doing with the condo and the stuff in it. All I had to do was get my personal items packed and shipped back here to Pryor and I had a month in which to do that.

Fax number? None at the motel. Maybe Ben has one at his store. Well, maybe that would not be a good idea. He is already very much involved with my family matters. Perhaps it would be best to check at the library, if, in fact Pryor even has a library.

I did find the library and asked if they had a fax machine I could use for a business transaction. They said "Yes, for a slight fee." I was happy to pay the "slight fee" to get the number I needed. And pay a slight fee for the use of the phone.

With that taken care of, and a return call to Marie, I had the rest of the day to go out to the farm to talk with Ron.

As I came out of the library I walked right in to Nurse Nancy, no, Nora, once again.

"It seems like I'm always running into you or spilling stuff on you or opening a door into you. Am I bad luck?" I asked her.

"No, you're not bad luck," she said. "As I told you once before, 'you're just hazardous!' Nevertheless, it's good to see you again. We thought for awhile that you had disappeared."

"Nope! Here I am, in the flesh!"

We both stood there on the library steps talking and laughing. "Wow", I thought, "She has a beautiful smile."

"Follow your heart!" "What?" *"Follow your heart!"*

"Uh, Nora," I stammered, "I know you are probably busy and have lots of things you could be doing or maybe even having to work or…oh, what the heck, would you be interested in having dinner with me some evening?"

"Well now, Mr. Edwards," she said, "that's a mighty fine invitation you have extended to me. As a matter of fact, I was just thinking of asking you the same thing. But, since you asked me first that means you have to pay, right? Right!"

"I'll give you a call," I said.   And, after a few more pleasantries, with that we both left the library and headed in separate directions. I headed back to the farm.

Ron was walking from the barn when I drove up to the farm house.   He seemed to be limping more than ever and stopping every few steps to catch his breath.

"Hi, Ron," I called out, "are you alright?"

"Yeah," he said, "I'm fine. Just a little tired from lack of sleep, I guess. By the way, where have you been? I checked around town for you this morning and no one seemed to know where you were."

I related the same story to Ron that I had told Ben back in town.

"I thought I would stop by and ask you if it would be okay for me to spend a few days with you here on the farm until I can find a place of my own," I said.

"Sure, that's what I wanted to tell you when I went all over town looking for you. I was going to ask if you wanted to stay here at the farm instead of the motel. You can stay here as long as you like. Just know that I won't be much company for you and you'll have to get your own meals."

"Ron, I've not come here asking you to take care of me. I want to help out as much as I can while I'm here. All you have to do is tell me what needs to be done and I'll make every effort to help you do it, get it done myself or hire somebody to do it."

"Lee, we've got to talk about the farm and what you want to do with it. I don't know how much longer I can keep it going. And too, there's the Feed and Seed Store in town. It's been closed ever since Clint Burdett absconded with the money and Gran had the stroke. I just don't have the energy or the desire to try to keep it going."

135

"Ron, come and set down here on the front porch with me."

We both went up the steps and sat on the porch swing where dad used to sit and rub Old True's head. It wasn't the same swing because the old one had been replaced with a newer and nicer one, but it was still hanging from the same iron rings in the same wooden beam that went from one end of the porch to the other

I glanced up at the beam. I remembered that it was the one my dad used to replace the one that was destroyed by the tornado that tore off our front porch when it passed through the area when I was a kid. That was such a long time ago, but I can still see him working to replace it.

As Ron and I sat on the swing, I noticed beads of perspiration on his face.

"Ron," I began, "I'm concerned about you. You don't look good. I think you've been working too hard trying to keep this place up."

"Don't be concerned about me," he said. "Now that you are here you can decide what you want to do with the farm and I will find me a place to live in town. I think maybe Ben can use me at the store and station. He suggested it some time ago."

"Ron, I need to tell you something important. The farm doesn't belong to me. It belongs to you. At least it will on the day you are twenty five."

"How can that be?" he replied. "You're Grandpa and Gran's only son. You are the heir to the farm. It's yours. It shouldn't be mine. To be completely honest, I'm not even sure I would want it."

"No, Ron, they remade their will and it states that when you are twenty five and they have not heard from me, the farm becomes yours. It is yours, and rightfully so. I want to honor their wishes."

"Lee, under normal conditions I would probably thank you for your generosity, but, as you can well see, I am in no condition to try to run this farm. And besides, it doesn't make enough to break even. I keep going in debt just to purchase feed for the few livestock we have left. I found out that Grandpa sold off livestock to cover the losses and pay the bills that were caused by Clint's embezzlement of the Feed and Seed Store resources.

"It seems like Grandpa's sudden death and Grandma's stroke and death sucked all desire out of me to keep it going. While they were alive I wanted to do everything I could to help them keep their hopes alive. Now I don't have any reason to do that anymore."

It was easy to see the discouragement and sense of defeat in his face. Tears began to form and he turned away, looking over the farmland that had been home to him for all but about two years of his life.

I noticed that his shoulders drooped a little more than before and he looked pale.

"No! No! No!" I said, as I placed my hand on his shoulder. "By golly, this is going to be your farm and you're going to make it work. You have poured your life into this place and you have kept it going. Now it's time for you to get to see some of the rewards of your work."

Ron looked straight at me and said, "How do you plan to make that happen since you live and work in Portland and I'm not able to keep going here?"

"First," I said, "I'm not going to be living in Portland. I've been fired from my job. At first I didn't know what I was going to do, but after being here and learning what needs to be done with the farm and feed store, I've decided that this is where I want to be. I want to be here .....here with you, that is, if you will have me."

"Lee, it may take me some time to get used to the idea of having a father around. Grandpa was a lot like a dad to me, but I think I kind of got used to the idea that I would never have a father, since I didn't know you and my step-dad didn't want me around. Maybe if you will give me some time I think I might be able to adjust to the idea."

"Ron, you take all the time you need. I really have no right to rush you into any kind of relationship with which you are not comfortable.

"Nevertheless, comfortable or not, we're going to do something about that hip of yours. Ben told me that you have avoided having something done about it because of the expense involved."

"Well," said Ron, "the cost is prohibitive and I don't have any insurance."

"That will be no concern of yours. I will soon have the financial resources to cover the cost, whatever it is, and we're going to get something done. I at least owe that to you.

"Next, we're going to work together to get this place up and running again like it did when dad and grandpa and great-grandpa worked it and made something of it.

"I may have been a jerk and done things in my life that did not dignify the Edward's name, but those days are over. I'm going to try to be the father that I should have been for these twenty five years and, hopefully, my son will accept my effort to be so."

"Lee," Ron said, "I don't know if I have the energy or the desire to go through the process of hip replacement – or if it is even possible. The doctors weren't too sure it could be done when we talked about it before."

I looked him straight in the eyes and could feel only love for this young man that I had known for only a week.

"Son," the word came straight from my heart.

"Follow your heart!"

"Son," I said a second time. And then there were no more words. I just looked into his face through tears that fell unashamedly onto my chest.

"Lee," he said, "I've wanted to call you dad from the very first. It didn't seem right to call you Lee, especially believing that you are my dad, but not really knowing you as a dad. I didn't know what to call you or if it would be okay with you if I did call you dad."

My own dad used to sit on this swing and stroke Old True while he laid his head on dad's knee. Now, sitting in this same swing, I found myself stroking the back of my grown son's head as it lay on my shoulder.

Time stood still! Now I sit here wondering what my child looked like when he was growing up; how he did in school; what sports he played; did he play a musical instrument; what kind of a student he was; how he combed his hair; did he like blue or brown; did he wash behind his ears? Did he like squash? Was he afraid in his room? Did he like to run and chase with a dog?

I will probably never know, for now he's a grown man.

I realized that I had missed so much, simply because I was afraid and I ran. I realized that my fear made me miss a lot of good things in my life, especially an adult relationship with my folks and a father's relationship with my son. Thinking back, I also sacrificed what could have been a good and long lasting relationship with his mother, even though we started in all the wrong ways.

Yes, I think I've always known that what Bonnie and I did was wrong. We were young and impulsive and I insisted that we express our love for each other in a wrong way.

However, here I set with the strong, kind and handsome young man who is the product of that relationship. How can I regret what happened?

What if she had aborted him? What a loss! What a tragedy!

But, she didn't!

.

CHAPTER 20

While living in Portland, I had come to develop a close friendship with a physician who had expertise in joint replacement. I made arrangements with Dr. Alfred Morgan-O'dell of the Fiester Medical Center in Portland for a thorough examination and recommendation for a possible hip replacement for Ron. The appointment for the exam was set within two weeks, shortly after Ron's twenty fifth birthday.

In the meantime, while waiting for time to take the trip to Portland, I arranged for a birthday party at the farm. We invited several of Ron's friends with whom he had attended school as well as some of the community people that had helped Ron on the farm following dad's death. The invitation also included Nurse Nora and some other caregivers from the Mary-Martha Nursing Home.

It turned out to be a very happy and lively occasion with lots of food, music and a little dancing in the living room.

Mrs. Orrin Webb, the pianist at the Pryor Community Church, agreed to provide music on the grand piano that had been covered up when I first came back to the house. Now it was uncovered, polished and looked like it did when I played on it when I was a kid.

Mrs. Webb was a really good pianist. If she played the church hymns with the same gusto with which she played the songs that night, they must have a rousing good time in their worship services. Even the Reverend Reinfeld could be seen tapping his feet in a lively fashion.

Ron seemed to enjoy himself immensely. He sat most of the evening and everyone came by to visit with him at one time or another before the party was over. By the time the festivities ended, however, it was evident that Ron had come to the end of his meager supply of energy.

"Ladies and gentlemen, may I have your attention," I said. "I know that Ron would like to thank all of you for coming to his birthday party, but it looks like he has just about enough energy left to make it to bed. Therefore, I'm going to declare an end to the festivities.

"However, before you leave I want to let all of you know that in the next couple of days Ron and I will be leaving to go to the Fiester Medical Center in Portland. Dr. Morgan-O'dell, a renowned orthopedic surgeon that I know" – *I simply couldn't help but mention that,* "is going to examine Ron's hip in order to determine if he can have a total hip replacement.

"I think all of you know that his hip was crushed in a car accident about five years ago. We have hopes that it can be corrected through replacement surgery.

"Ron and I wish to thank all of you who have come tonight, but also to thank those of you who have agreed to keep an eye on the farm while we are gone. We will be in touch with you to let you know what happens."

Friends and neighbors began to disperse from the house, get into their cars and start home. Ron and I stood on the front porch waving goodbye and endeavoring to greet each one before they left.

Nora was the last to leave. When she stepped up beside us on the porch she asked, "When did you say you are leaving for Portland?"

I answered, "Ron and I thought that we would be leaving in the next two or three days because it will take us about that long to get there, depending on how well Ron rides. It's a long and tiring trip."

Ron excused himself because he was tired and said that he was going to his room and go to bed.

When we had said goodnight to him, Nora asked, "Since you're leaving does that mean that you are not planning on taking me out to dinner, like you promised? I've been waiting for you to call. You said you would."

"Nora," I said, somewhat embarrassed, "I am so sorry. I know it sounds awful, but to tell you the truth I got so wrapped up in getting help for Ron and making arrangements for him to see the orthopedic surgeon, the dinner invitation totally slipped my mind. I'm sorry, I forgot."

"Well," she said, "I've been stood up before and this probably won't be the last time, so do what you have to do. If and when you ever get back to Pryor, maybe you can work me into your busy schedule. I have to go to work. I was called in for the nightshift." Then she turned and walked out to her car.

I followed part way down the walk and called "Nora." But she did not stop or turn around. I stood at the edge of the yard and watched as she got into her car and drove away.

She was very hurt. I heard it in her voice and the fact that she didn't respond when I called out to her. I felt that awful sickening feeling in the pit of my stomach; the kind you get when you know you have done something wrong, but there is no way to undo it. I really was looking forward to having dinner with her when we first talked about it.

"Were you? Then why did you do the same thing all over again?"

"What 'same thing' again?" I found myself asking.

"You sabotaged your heart. You were doing pretty well at following your heart for awhile, but then you went back figuring out ways to avoid getting involved in a personal relationship with a woman."

"What do you mean by that?"

"Well, for example, you took control with Ron's situation. Did you even inquire of Ron what he wanted to do about a possible surgery or did you just decide that was what he was going to do? Did you ask him if he wanted a birthday party and invite the people you did? Are you doing all this in an effort to make up for all the lost years you avoided finding out about him?

"No," I said, "It just seems to me that the right thing to do is help him get a hip replacement so that he can function without pain and live the rest of his life in some state of normalcy."

"And why the sudden interest in his welfare?"

"Because he's my son," I said.

"He's been your son for twenty five years and you've done nothing about it in all that time."

"Well, I said, "this is now and I know him and I want to do something to help him."

"Is that the way it is or are you using your sudden interest his welfare as a reason for not establishing a relationship with Nora? Did you forget you invited her out to dinner or did you purposely push it out of your mind to avoid a relationship with her like you have done with all the other women in your life?"

"Get off my back and get out of my life," I yelled.

"I can't. I'm an essential part of who you are and if you deny me it could wind up killing you."

"Where have I heard that line before? Have you been talking with my mom?"

"You are at a crossroads, Lee. Either you follow your heart and be vulnerable or keep running and miss out on what relationships are all about. That will be true with both Ron and Nora, or, for that matter, anyone else with whom you desire to relate. If you desire normalcy in your own life, think about it."

I stood there watching Nora's car go down the lane and saw the brake lights as she stopped and then turned right onto the main road that goes into Pryor. I slowly walked back up to the house and sat down on the porch swing. It was too late and too dark to walk down to the lake where I seem to be able to do my best thinking, so I sat down in the swing.

What *is* my motive for helping Ron get his hip fixed? Why did I forget the dinner invitation and the promise to call Nora?

"Follow your heart. What would you really like to do?"

I immediately got up from the swing, went back in the house to the phone and called her at work. She had the night shift. "Hi. Nora, this is Lee. Ron and I won't be leaving for Portland for a couple of days. Would you still be interested in going to dinner with me before we leave? I would be paying, of course.

"I'm sorry, Lee," she said, "but I've already made other plans."

"Oh, you've already made other plans?" *That was quick,* I thought "Okay. Well maybe we can get together when Ron and I get back from Portland. Okay? Well, sorry to interrupt your work, bye."

"Why do you give up so easily? Why do you find it so easy to do something that you have made up your mind about, such as arranging for Ron to go to Portland for a hip replacement, but when

Nora says she is not free to have dinner with you, you give up and make no effort to get her to change her mind?"

"Well," I insisted, "she said she had other plans."

"And you believe her? Is that what is stopping you from insisting on going out to dinner or it is your way of getting out of it altogether?"

I really do like her and I really would like to go out to dinner with her and I really would like to get to know her better. So, what *is* keeping me from insisting...from insisting......insisting? Oh!"

"What, Lee?" What are you thinking?"

"It seems like that is what I did with Bonnie all those years ago. I *insisted* that we do what we did even though she believed it wasn't right. I *insisted* that it was because we loved one another, but deep inside I know I was thinking only about what I wanted. in order to gratify one of my needs and so I kept *insisting* that it happen.

She gave in to my insistence and as a result my insistence ruined our relationship. That same insistence has ruined several other relationships with women since then. Consequently, I haven't trusted myself to establish a positive relationship with women for all these years for fear of messing up the same way I did with Bonnie."

"Lee, you have allowed what happened over twenty five years ago to impact the rest of your life and all of your relationships, especially with women. When are you going to forgive yourself for what happened then and get on with your life?"

"Forgive myself? How can I forgive myself for what I did to Bonnie and for ignoring Ron all these years? How can I forgive myself for hurting my parents like I did by running away and never being in touch with them and making them have to raise my child? That's un-forgivable. I can't do it."

"*Remember what your mother told Ron when he was holding on to his bitterness and resentment that he had toward you? Remember?*"

"Yes. How could anyone forget?" She said, 'Ron, if you hold on to your un-forgiveness it will kill you.' That was always her clincher."

"*She was right, you know? Your parents forgave you. Ron has forgiven you. It's time you forgave yourself.*"

Forgive myself? Well, it sounded a strange thing to forgive myself for all the stuff that came to my mind. I did it. Then I realized it was no more strange than talking to myself all the time anyhow. The only difference is that when I finished I felt different.

I sat there on that porch swing and forgave myself for what I did to Bonnie, for running away and failing to accept my part and my responsibility for Ron's birth, for abandoning both Bonnie and Ron, for the way I treated my folks by rebelling and running away and never being in touch with them, for wanting to maim or kill Clint Burdett for destroying my folks business by taking their money, for telling my boss off when he fired me, for failing to remember to call Nora like I promised and for every other thing that surfaced from deep inside me that had been buried for so long.

Then I remembered what Ron had said my mom had told him, which also reminded me that she had told me the same thing many times, but I ignored it: "get rid of the bitterness in your heart; the rage and anger, the brawling and slander and the malice that you have there. You need to be kind and compassionate, forgiving just like you have been forgiven. Otherwise, it'll kill you." She never seemed to let that one pass.

I couldn't remember where mom had learned all those little sermons in a sentence. Probably in church. When I was a kid and went with them to church I never really paid all that much attention.

"Perhaps you should have. It may have been good for you."

"Yes, conscience or heart or spirit or whatever part of me you are, I think you may be right."

It was even later now, but I phoned her anyhow. "Nora, I know it's late and I know you are at work and I know you probably don't want to see me, but I want to come over to see you. I will be there in about twenty minutes. I need to talk with you. Bye."

I didn't give her time to say no or refuse my visit. Was this another case of manipulating or insisting? Perhaps, but for an entirely different reason!

The meeting with Nora was a little uncomfortable at first, but after I asked her to forgive me for being so insensitive to her, she finally warmed up a bit and agreed to have dinner with me the next night, providing I pay as I promised. I said I would.

She took a twenty minute break from her work and we walked out into the cool evening air. I found myself continuing to apologize for my insensitivity.

"Lee, why don't we not waste my break time with me having to tell you over and over again 'it's alright, I forgive you?' You had other things on your mind and I know that now. So, let's enjoy what little time we have and just be friends. Okay?"

"Yes, Nora," I said, as I almost slipped and apologized once again for bringing it up. I didn't. So I just said, "Okay."

The twenty minutes flew by quickly. She had to return to her work and I went to my car for the return trip to the farm.

When I arrived at the farm house, only one small light was on at the bottom of the stairs. Ron had already retired and the house was quiet. I sat on the swing for awhile and looked up at the starlit sky that also revealed only a sliver of moon. It was a beautiful night just to sit and think about all the things that were happening in my life within the last two weeks, especially what could be developing into a relationship with Nora – a totally new kind of relationship for me.

I finally turned off the light, climbed the stairs in the darkness and went to my room. Sleep came easily with no shadowy figures slithering from under my bed.

It seemed that all the lust, the fear and the anger no longer had any place to reside – at least in me.

CHAPTER 21

Early the next morning I stopped by Ben's convenience store to pick up some items I needed for the house.

"I'm glad you stopped in, Lee."

"What is it, Ben?" I asked

"Well," said Ben, "Fred Powers, an attorney friend of mine over in Fayetteville, called early this morning to inquire if we still have a Burdett family living here in Pryor. I told him that the Burdetts own a farm and have lived here for as long as I have been here – almost fifty years.

"He said that he had been asked by one of the businesses in town to run a background check on a person who has made application for a job with their firm. The last name is Burdett and he thought he remembered us talking about the name one time in a conversation we had and was wondering if somehow they might be related.

"He also thought he remembered that a Jerry Burdett had been Sheriff of this county at one time. I told him that he remembered correctly."

"Ben," I asked, "what is all this leading up to?"

"Well, patience, Lee. I'm getting to it. You will be interested in this. My friend wanted to know if I knew Clint Burdett. I said I did, but it has been almost five years since he left town and I hadn't seen or heard anything of him since. "

"He said he was running the background check on Clint and was wondering if I knew of anything that would prevent him from being hired on with a particular business.

"I was curious, so I asked him what kind of business is it for which he is making application? And he said that it was to be a business manager and accountant for a savings and loan company in Fayetteville. He has a Business Administration degree listed on his resume."

"That *is* interesting." I said. "Small world, isn't it? It seems that no matter how far you run, your past ultimately catches up with you. I, for one, should know!"

Ben just paused and looked at me for a long minute.

"Anyhow," continued Ben, "I told my friend, as a matter of fact, Fred, there are some very good reasons why Clint should not be given an okay for that position. In the first place he worked for the Edwards family business here in Pryor and embezzled several thousands of dollars before the books were audited and the loss was discovered.

"Even more than that, we suspect that he is the hit and run driver that committed vehicular homicide, killing Mr. Edwards and crippling their grandson. We believe that the car accident was deliberately covered up by his uncle, Jerry Burdett, who helped Clint leave town and then disappeared himself when the people did not re-elect him as Sheriff.

"I told Fred that he may well want to talk with the local police and have them arrest Clint for embezzlement for sure and also suspicion of vehicular homicide. He said he would take steps to do that and thanked me for the information."

151

"Ben, thanks for telling me this," I said. "Maybe now there can be some kind of closure to my folks' death and also a solution as to what to do with the business. Is there still a possibility that Clint can be taken to court and some kind of restitution made for the money he embezzled?"

"Yes, Lee," Ben replied, "I think there can be some kind of settlement and restitution. Your folks had a good insurance policy on both the farm and the Feed Store. Perhaps now the insurance company can go to court and settle accounts with Clint and company."

"However," he continued, "there is still the greater issue of the hit and run that caused your dad's death. If Clint is responsible for that, the embezzlement problem will seem like small potatoes to him. He could wind up with some serious jail time.

"I feel sorry for his folks," Ben continued. "They are good people and have always tried their best to be there for their kids. Clint really had great potential all through school and when he first came back to Pryor. Somewhere along the way I guess he let greed and selfish-ambition take over his life."

Deep in my thoughts came the realization, *"Lee, you, of all people, should be able to understand how that can happen."*

"Yeah," I said, "I think I can understand a little of how that can happen."

"Call me, Ben, if anything else shows up on this. Okay? I'll be out at the farm if you need me."

"Sure, Lee. I'll do that."

I went back out to the farm and got ready for a very important meeting. I wasn't about to forget the occasion again.

CHAPTER 22

I stopped by and picked up Nora for dinner. I arrived about half an hour early. Maybe it was a little sense of guilt from having forgotten the first invitation or maybe I was really eager to have some time with her. Either way, she seemed to be pleased that I even showed up at all. She was ready ahead of time.

I had the top down on the convertible because it was such a warm, beautiful evening. I thought perhaps we could drive in to the city, about twenty five miles away, and eat at a very upscale Giraffe Bar restaurant that used to be there.

However, she directed me to a small but cozy cafe that she knew about on the outskirts of Pryor and suggested that we go there because they served good food at a reasonable price. I wanted to splurge, again probably to deal with my guilty conscience, but the place she chose turned out to be a really good place to eat.

We were seated at a corner table near the fireplace. In a few minutes someone came and lit a fire in it. Not that one was needed, for it was still around seventy degrees at seven p.m. I think the owners wanted to create a certain ambiance for Nora and the guy she brought to dinner with her.

The waitress came and took our order for drinks. Both of us asked for sweet tea and a glass of water, hers without lemon, mine with. When the waitress brought the drinks, Nora flashed that million dollar smile once again as she took the first sip of her tea and gave an 'aaaaah' sigh. It was good sweet tea. We both laughed as we mentioned the commercial where a person is falling backwards into a swimming pool filled with iced tea.

After giving us time to look over the menu the waitress returned and took our orders. Nora ordered an oriental chicken salad, and that was it. No meat. No potatoes. No dessert, just oriental chicken salad.

My appetite craved for more than salad, so I ordered shrimp scampi, mashed potatoes, steamed vegetables, garlic seasoned bread and bread pudding for dessert. She will probably sleep well tonight. I will probably turn and toss all night while my stomach and intestines growl at me for forcing them to digest such a heavy load.

Nevertheless, the dinner time was very enjoyable. The conversation was pleasant and smiles and laughter were seen and heard throughout the meal.

We talked of when and why she had arrived in Pryor. I found out that she came about ten years after I had left town and knew nothing of me except for some tidbits that had been picked up in conversation with people in various places around town. She had really come to know me only when I first visited the nursing home to see my mother, about two or three weeks ago.

She had heard of a need for nurses in the Mary Martha Nursing Home and came to Pryor primarily in answer to that need. She had desired to move away from where she lived before and the new job seemed like an excellent opportunity to have that happen. She never revealed to me why she desired to leave where she lived before. I did not press the issue.

I shared some about going to Maine to look for work, my brief adventure with the lobster fishing expedition, and ultimately working as a paralegal with a law firm in Portland.

She never inquired as to why I left Pryor in the first place and I saw no need to go into the details about it. I had already surmised that based on the circumstances of our meetings at the nursing home, mom's memorial service and the various conversations that occurred between her, Ron and me, she had already come to a conclusion. I did not need to explain it.

This dinner was about us, Nora and me.

The time sped by and before we realized it we were the last couple left in the café before closing time at eleven p.m. As soon as I paid the bill we exited the café and the doors were locked behind us. When we heard the click of the lock and saw the OPEN sign turned over to CLOSED, we looked at each other and grinned.

The drive to Nora's place was warm and pleasant. We talked mostly of how much we had enjoyed each other's company and how we may want to do it again sometime in the near future – like tomorrow night. That was her night to work so we agreed to do it again later in the week. But that would be difficult to do before Ron and I left for Portland. We realized that we had to leave sooner than that, so plans were made for a get together upon our return from Portland.

I watched her as she walked to the door of her cottage, open it, turn on the lights and turn to wave goodbye to me. I had felt no inclination to invite myself in, nor did she invite me. There was no need.

I began to drive back out to the farm, ready for a good night's sleep with good dreams of a great evening with a special lady.

"You have reached a new milestone, haven't you?"

"What do you mean?"

"You enjoyed Nora's company throughout the evening without the slightest thought of anything other than being with her as a friend. You did not insist on anything else."

"Nora is a beautiful person and I had no need to insist that she be anything else. Yes, I think I've reached a new milestone; in fact, I know I have."

"Feels good, doesn't it?"

"As a matter of fact, yes, it does!"

I pulled up in front of the farmhouse, parked the car and began to walk toward the front porch.

"Lee," called Ron from the top of the stairs, "Ben has been trying to get in touch with you much of the evening. I told him I did not know where you were, except that you and Nora had gone out to dinner."

"Did he say what he wanted, Ron?" I asked.

"No,' answered Ron, "he just said that it was important and that you and he talked about it earlier today. He wanted you to give him a call however late it was when you got back."

"Thanks, Ron," I said, "I'll phone him now."

I went into the kitchen, picked up the phone and dialed Ben's number at his home. "Ben, this is Lee. You've been trying to get hold of me this evening?"

"Yes, I have, but Ron said that you and Nora had gone out for the evening and he didn't know how to get hold of you."

"Yeah, Nora and I went out to dinner and I just got back a few minutes ago. What's up?"

"Lee, Fred wants to come to Pryor and talk with us about Clint Burdett?"

"When?"

"Tomorrow night."

"Tomorrow night? Wow, Ron and I are trying to get out of town as soon as possible to make the appointment with Dr. Odell in Portland."

"I know you are, Lee, but he's willing to drive all the way here if you and Ron are available."

"Ben, that's a long way to come. It must be over two hundred miles. What time?"

"He wants to meet us at 7 o'clock."

"Okay Ben, I'll plan to be at your place then. Thanks. Goodnight."

I hung up the phone and walked up the stairs toward my room.

"Lee, may I ask what Ben wanted," Ron asked. "He seemed awfully anxious to get hold of you for some reason. I was just wondering what it was. Is everything okay?"

"Sure is Ron," I said. "Ben talked with me this morning about a lawyer friend of his in Fayetteville who was doing a back-ground check on someone who was applying for a job. That "someone" turned out to be Clint Burdett.

"Ben's friend is coming to Pryor tomorrow evening for a meeting with him and with you and me, if we can postpone our trip one day. He wants to find out where to go from here in dealing with Clint's embezzlement. He also wants to discuss the possibility of him being the one who rammed into dad's pickup. Are you up to such a meeting?"

Ron answered, "I think so. I'm still feeling kind of weak, but if this will bring some kind of resolution to Grandpa and Gran's death and for the farm and business they worked so hard to establish, I guess the least I can do is make every effort to be in on it."

My night's sleep turned out to be a mix of pleasant dreams about Nora, and dealing with a vengeful attitude toward Clint Burdett.

Ron and I spent the next morning taking care of the livestock, mucking out the stalls, milking the few cows that were left and turning them out to pasture. I could easily see why it was so difficult for Ron to manage taking care of the animals. It is hard to walk with a crutch and shovel manure at the same time.

It felt good for me to be doing some physical labor again and to work up a sweat while doing it. How long had it been since that has happened to me? It has been several years, at least. Not since the time when I worked the Lobster pots off the coast of Maine. My muscles will cry out in pain by the end of the day, of that I can be sure.

Ron had talked with Ted Russell about staying on the farm and taking care of the animals while he and I were in Portland for his possible surgery. Ted and his parents lived on a farm about five miles down the road from our place. He was about Ron's age and they had grown up together, going through school and both learning farming from their parents, or in Ron's case, grandparents.

Ted agreed to take care of the farm and moved in to one of the rooms in the farmhouse, one in which he had stayed over with Ron on lots of occasions. It was like home to him. And, I'm sure in the same way that Ted's place seemed like home to Ron. They were very close friends; kind of like brothers.

Ted took care of the evening chores while Ron and I went to the meeting with Ben and Mr. Powers. We were eager to find out what he knew about Clint and what had been done to make sure he didn't disappear again before something could be done to make him face up to the embezzlement and also the wreck that killed my dad.

We met in a room in the back of Ben's convenience store. He called it his office. It looked more like an army surplus store.

"Fred," said Ben, "this is Lee Edwards and Ron Edwards. They are CJ and Melissa Edwards' son and grandson. CJ and Melissa were the ones who owned the Feed and Seed Store where Clint Burdett worked and where he embezzled money from the business."

"Good to meet you gentlemen," said Mr. Powers. "I guess Ben has already told you about the conversation we had yesterday regarding Clint. I was just doing a usual background check on him when I happened across the information that Ben shared with me about what happened when he worked for your folks."

"Yes," I replied, "he has told us about your conversation and, I must say, we are both surprised and pleased that Clint has turned up again. It's been a long five years and things have been tough, especially at the Feed and Seed Store, which is now closed."

Fred said, "I'm sorry that you and your folks have had to be faced with this, but perhaps we can help get things straightened out. Clint has been arrested and is now confined in the Fayetteville city jail and will be held there until formal charges are made by you. I assume that you will want to file charges for embezzlement."

Ron and I looked at each other and without discussing anything we both spoke at the same time, "We certainly do wish to file charges now."

Ben suggested that we hire Fred to be our attorney and to be the one to contact the insurance company to notify them that the embezzler had been caught and is now in jail. It will be up to the insurance company to work out the details with the court on how to handle the case and what kind of restitution is to be made. We agreed.

As to the matter of the hit and run vehicular homicide charge, Fred suggested that we allow one of the investigators that he has working for him look in to the details of the accident report that was handled by the local Sheriff's department when Jerry Burdett was Sheriff. He will discover whether a report was filed and also what happened to the hit and run vehicle. Most likely he will want to interview persons here in Pryor who have any remembrance of the accident, especially those of us who went to the scene shortly after it happened. Again, we agreed.

The meeting did not last more than an hour, but we all felt that it was very productive and steps had been initiated to begin the process of clearing up all the loose ends related to both my dad's death and also the matter of embezzlement of money from the store.

With those matters clearly in the hands of persons who knew how to handle them, Ron and I went back to the farm and began making preparations to leave early in the morning for Portland and, hopefully, a new future for him.

One more call, however, needed to be made. I needed to talk with Nora.

"Nora, this is Lee."

"Oh, hi Lee. How are you doing?"

"I'm fine, Nora. How about you?"

"They called me in to work the day shift today. Seems a friend of mind kept me up late a couple of nights ago."

"You had to work today? Wow, you must be worn out. Sorry about that. No, I'm not sorry about keeping you out late. Sorry you had to work today."

"It's okay, Lee. Don't worry about it. I will survive."

"Nora, I will need to take a rain check on our plans for our next dinner together. I just wanted to call and apologize. It is necessary for Ron and me to leave early tomorrow morning in order to be in Portland on Friday to meet with the Dr. about his possible surgery.

"It's okay, Lee. You two have a safe trip. I'll see you when you get back."

"Thanks for being so understanding. I'll call you when we get there and also let you know when we are coming back. Okay? Thanks. And Nora, thanks again for the great time we had together the other night.

"I really enjoyed it Lee. Thanks for taking me to dinner. I had fun."

"Me too. Bye."

I went to bed still thinking of how much I enjoy talking with Nora and how badly I truly felt about the fact that she had had a really hard day at work. I felt like I was actually beginning to care about her and was sorry to have to be away from her for who knows how long.

Following my heart may not be such a bad idea after all

CHAPTER 23

I spent a lot of time thinking about the ordeal that Ron faced with a possible hip replacement. At the same time I realized that I still held on to that vengeful attitude that I had toward Clint Burdett. He really deserves to get what's coming to him for all the misery he caused my family.

"Yes, I suppose he really does deserve to get what's coming to him."

But, at the same time, it keeps gnawing at my mind, is what he did any worse than what I did to them? I didn't steal their money or hurt them physically. But I did steal twenty five years of happiness from them and hurt them emotionally because they never knew what happened to me. I robbed them of a relationship with their only son. Which is the greater form of embezzlement?

I had to ask myself the question, *"What do you think you deserve to get for your own form of embezzlement and emotional wreckage that you perpetrated against your folks?"*

I don't know. Since the day I learned that they had forgiven me for what I did, I have felt different about my life. Their forgiveness set me free somehow. I know it didn't erase what I did or excuse what I did, but it did lift a heavy burden off my shoulders – and my heart.

Knowing that is what they did for me, I was able to forgive myself and take on a whole new attitude toward my life. I feel different because of it. I am different.

I had to wonder if the same thing could happen to Clint if he were forgiven for what he did.

"Why don't you try it?"

There goes that heart thing again.

"Try it?" I asked, "Do you mean forgive him for the actual embezzlement of their money? Or, what about the wreck that killed my dad and injured my son? That's asking an awful lot. What would happen with the charges that have been filed if we were to forgive him?

"Nothing! Clint will have to face up to the responsibility he had for what happened in both cases. Forgiveness does not excuse his acts of irresponsibility. It only sets you free from the vengeful attitude you have toward him and the bitterness that you are storing up in your heart against him. That could ultimately kill you, you know."

Where have I heard that before? "You've been talking to mom again!"

"And too, your forgiveness of Clint could well set him free from his acts of rebellion and irresponsibility and then he may be able to accomplish some of the potential that he has in his life. It happened with you."

That, it did. It most certainly did. I will talk with Ron about it, but not tonight. We'll do it tomorrow on our way to Portland.

It had been a very long day and sleep came easily. Even my newly exercised and sore muscles did not hesitate long enough to complain about being overworked. They joined in the sleep with a sigh of relief.

We were up early the next morning, having a breakfast that Ron had prepared, putting our stuff into the car and getting ready for the long two or three day trip to Portland.

As we sat at the table I asked, "Ron, is this something you really want to do? I guess I just assumed that you would be happy about the possibility of getting your hip fixed and never took time to even inquire if that is what you want to happen. I didn't mean to just drop back into town and start to take over your life. You're not a little kid. You are a grown man who has been making your own decisions for a long time. You don't need me to make them for you."

"That's okay, dad, I don't mind. I think it took someone to get me off dead center and also make me quit feeling sorry for myself. I still have a lot of hatred for the guy that rammed grandpa's pickup, killed him and put me in this shape. I'm still seething over what Clint did with their money from the store."

"Me, too, Ron. I also have a lot of hatred for that person who rammed into the pickup. The only one I can think of that did it, is Clint Burdett. I've been dealing with some major feelings of vengeance toward him and I'm struggling with how to handle it. I didn't even know where in the world he might be, but I kept thinking if I could just get my hands on him."

"Dad, one time a guy did something to me here in town that really made me mad and I wanted to work him over and beat the daylights out of him. I was so angry Grandma could see that it was ruining my health so she said, 'Ron, holding un-forgiveness in our hearts is kind of like us drinking poison and hoping that it will kill someone else.' I never forgot that."

"I think if I continue to hold hatred in my heart toward Clint for his embezzlement and for whoever caused the wreck, it will be like Grandma said, I'm drinking the poison hoping it will kill Clint."

"She was a wise woman, wasn't she, Ron?"

"She sure was!"

We knew what we had to do before we could expect anything good to come out of our trip to Portland. Setting at the breakfast table, Ron and I – father and son, spoke words of forgiveness for Clint and his embezzlement from the store. We also asked God to forgive us for our hatred of him and our desire to work vengeance on him.

Both of us knew that we had done the right thing. Now we felt we could maybe deal with it without being distraught and ruled by our emotions. At least that's what we hoped would happen. Only time would tell!

CHAPTER 24

The day was beautiful and warm. We did not put the top down on the convertible because we had the back seat packed with whatever we thought we might need for our stay in Portland.

We were both silent for a long time, just looking at the scenery or farmlands, grazing animals, rolling hills and green pastures.

I broke the silence. "Ron, I have hesitated to say anything about this since you and I first started talking about our relationship. You may not want to talk about it or answer any questions, but if not, just tell me, okay?"

"What is it?"

"Has your mother stayed in touch with you at all through the years after you came to live with mom and dad?"

"I don't mind answering the question," he responded. "At first, when they were in town, mom would come by to see me. Even though Grandpa and Gran loved me a lot, I really missed my mom. I thought at first that she didn't want me or like me, but when I was a little older Gran helped me to understand what happened. At the same time, I really missed her and couldn't understand why she didn't come and get me.

"She sent me a birthday card and Christmas present for the first two or three years. Then those stopped. One time she called me just to see how I was doing. I felt so good knowing that she cared enough to call. I think I was about seven or eight at the time. But by that time I had begun to forget about her. It was almost like talking to a stranger.

"She tried to explain to me why she was not able to stop and see me anymore or send me cards and presents. Her husband didn't like me because he wasn't my father, and they had kids of their own. It's been fifteen or sixteen years since I have heard from her or have any knowledge of where they are. I think he is still driving eighteen wheelers and hauling stuff across the country. Last I heard they lived in Arlington, Texas, but I have never tried to get in touch with them."

"Thank you, Ron, I know it is a painful thing to bring up old memories. You were abandoned by both your father and mother. We were both kids without any knowledge of how to be a father or mother. I failed, because I was afraid and ran away. She at least gave you birth and tried to work and make a home for you with mom and dad's help. I not only failed you, I failed her as well. I pray that someday she will find it in her heart to forgive me."

We shared a lot of other things about Bonnie, how we met in school, rode horses together at the farm, picnicked at the lake and swam in it when the weather was hot and all the other things that young people enjoy doing together. It felt good to reminisce with Ron about the beautiful qualities that I had enjoyed in his mother.

Had it not been for my lustful insistence with her and the fear and anger that made me run away to forget, we may have enjoyed a good life together with our son.

Various other conversations and other long periods of silence accompanied us across the country for the two day and one night trip. We finally arrived in Portland Maine in time for the Dr.'s appointment on Friday morning.

I had gotten to know Dr. Morgan O'dell when we were in college together. While I was meandering through the various courses in an effort to decide what kind of a degree I desired to achieve, he, on the other hand had his mind set on being an orthopedic surgeon. He was single-minded in that endeavor and graduated from the university with top honors. He entered immediately into medical school and ultimately completed his training and residency program, also with top honors.

He was the first person I thought about when we began thinking of hip replacement for Ron. That's when I called him to see if it would be possible to make an appointment for him to see us and give an evaluation concerning Ron's hip. He agreed that it would, so that is why we're in his office now. It is good to see him and greet him again, now in a very nice office complex in one of the suburbs of Portland.

"Morgan," I said, "This is my son, Ron. He is the one I talked with you about regarding a hip replacement.

"Hi Ron," Morgan said as he shook his hand. "I am glad to meet you and I'm also glad to have the opportunity to take a look at that hip of yours to see what can be done to improve its function. Your dad has told me a lot about you in our conversations regarding your possible surgery. I am looking forward to getting to know you myself."

"Thank you, Dr. O'dell," Ron said. "I've been living with this hip for quite a few years. It would be nice if something can be done about it to get it working properly again.

"We'll certainly see what we can do, Ron," Morgan replied. "Now, let's talk about possibilities."

After a one hour consultation, followed by a series of X-rays and CT scans, which results came back a few days later, Dr. O'dell said that, up to this point, the prognosis was quite good for a successful hip replacement. However, some of the shattered bones had not healed properly, because the metal plates and screws had moved some since being used to hold the bones in place. Fortunately these could be replaced by the new hip unit.

He also indicated that there were some other things that showed up on the scans they were not quite sure about, nothing to really worry about he thought, but should be looked at when they did the surgery. I was particularly interested in what that might be, but was reassured that I should not worry about it.

Arrangements were made for surgery to be done on the following Friday, one week after our arrival in Portland. I thought that, in itself, was a kind of miracle - to get the surgery so soon after a consultation. However, I guess it pays to know people who know people.

In the meantime, I was still owner of a condo that was in the process of being sold. I still had access to it for another two weeks until the new owners took possession.

I had called Marie, my mortgage lady, to let her know I was going to be in town and wanted to stay in the condo for two weeks while Ron was having surgery. I had assured her that I would have all my personal belongings out of the condo by the end of the month.

Ron and I had settled in the condo when we first arrived and I had phoned Nora to let her know we had arrived and also how the meeting with the Dr. went. She thanked me and said that she was happy we had a safe and uneventful trip.

It may have been a safe trip, but it certainly was not an uneventful one. The sharing that we did during those two days and nights went a long way in helping us get to know each other. It was very eventful for both of us.

CHAPTER 25

Marie said she was glad to hear from me and asked if I could stop by the office to meet and talk with the prospective buyers Mr. & Mrs. Delbert Ross. I told her I would be happy to do that. We met on Monday of the following week with Marie and the Rosses.

Fortunately I had remembered to bring the papers that she had faxed to me at the Pryor library which had included the agreed upon price and the amount of the earnest money that had been paid to her.

When we met I discovered that the buyers had suddenly had second thoughts about the price they had agreed upon for the condo. They thought they were offering too much and began to name things they had found wrong with the place that should be fixed before they closed the agreement.

The condo was in immaculate condition when I bought it and it may have seen its periods of total disarray because it happened to be occupied by a working bachelor, but it had been kept in good repair, all the appliances were working and I had even purchased a new refrigerator within the last six months.

The location was ideal for a couple who desired to live near their work in downtown Portland. Housing prices had increased considerably and the market was good.

Nevertheless, they insisted that there were repairs that needed to be done and we agreed that we would all go together to see what those were. Fortunately, during the three days Ron and I had occupied the condo he had cleaned it until it sparkled as if Mom Edwards herself had stopped in for a housecleaning. It was spotless.

Nothing of significance was found that needed repaired, repainted or re-polished. In the course of examining the condo it became evident that they had most likely seen another condo that they liked better and wanted to get out of their agreement on this one. They kept comparing this and that with others that they had seen in other condos.

I reminded them that they were the ones who insisted on buying in the first place, I had agreed upon the price they offered, they had put down their earnest money and the preliminary papers had been signed.

The handsome check that I had envisioned being delivered at the closing of the sale appeared to be floating out the window. It would have certainly come in handy to help with the expenses of Ron's surgery.

About the time I was ready to acquiesce to the fact that they were not going to go through with the agreement, Ron spoke up,

"Dad," he said, "I think you ought to give them back their earnest money and let them go find another place that they can pick apart in hopes of being able to tell their friends how they were able to work a deal and get a real bargain for themselves.

"When I was with Dr. O'dell today for my consultation, he asked where you and I were staying. I told him at your condo until the first of the month when the new buyers were taking possession. He said he wanted to talk with you."

"Why?" I asked him. "Did he say what he wanted to talk about."

"Well," Ron said, "When I mentioned the condo he just said he was interested in talking with you."

"Now wait a minute," the Rosses interrupted, "we are the process of negotiating ourselves for this condo and what is this about a Dr. O'dell wanting to buy it?

"You may not be the only ones interested in it," Ron continued. "And besides, you seem, in fact, to have lost interest in it."

"You know, folks," he continued talking to the Rosses, "I grew up in a place where people shook hands when they came to an agreement and I was taught by people with integrity that that handshake was better than any piece of paper on which an agreement was written. It was written down only because the state required it.

"It is evidently different with you people who live here in the city. You appear to be the kind of people who get all excited about something you want. You sign papers and even pay money down on it; but when it comes right down to it, if you think you've found something better or find enough things wrong with what you wanted in the first place in order to get a better price than what you agreed on, all you have to do is say "sorry" and walk away.

"You're the ones who wanted the condo. You're the ones who had to have all the furniture left in the condo. You're the ones who wanted to be able to move in within thirty days. You're the ones who were eager to pay the earnest money. From what I understand, you initiated the whole thing."

"Listen," Shirley Ross said, "you don't have to be rude and insulting with us. We were only trying to get the best possible property for our money. Is there anything wrong with that?"

"No," Ron said, "I am not insulting you or being rude. And there is nothing wrong with making a good deal. The issue is, you made a good deal in the first place and you were happy with it; and now when it's time to close the deal you want to make a better one. I'm not insulting you. I'm simply questioning your integrity."

"We'll think about it," they said, as they turned and left the condo, with Marie, Ron and me standing there in the middle of this sparkling clean living room looking at each other, with me thinking, "I wish I had had the guts to tell them that."

"Dad," Ron said, "I am sorry if I messed up the closing of the deal on your condo. Their attitude just irritated me and I couldn't help myself."

"Don't worry about it Ron," I said. "Like mom used to say, "Just have faith and it will all work out okay."

"She said that to you too, huh?" Ron asked.

"Yes. You, too?"

"Yes!."

In some matters, it became evident that for mom, one size fits all.

Ron and I said "good night" to Marie as she exited shortly after the would-be buyers left to think about it. We shrugged our shoulders, rolled our eyes toward the ceiling and decided it was time to turn in for the night. We'll talk about it tomorrow.

After Marie left, Ron turned to me and said, "Dad, I really don't think Dr. O'dell is interested in buying the condo. I think he was interested in talking with you about my upcoming surgery and something he saw on the CT scan. He just said he wanted to talk with you. I think the Rosses understood it to mean that he wanted to talk with you about buying the condo. I didn't feel inclined to let them think otherwise, considering their bickering about the price and repairs and all."

"Ron," I said with a sense of pride in him, "you are amazing. You are something special! You are sharp! With the ability you just showed, you could be a real estate agent – or maybe even a card shark!"

We laughed together and each went to our own room to retire for the evening. I noticed that he looked a little weary as he walked to his room. It had been a long trip, an exhausting series of talks and tests with doctors and an explosive encounter with the Rosses. He had every right to be weary.

When I turned the light on in my bedroom, I immediately spotted a folded piece of paper laying on my pillow. I picked it up, unfolded it and saw that it was a note from Ron. It read:

"Dear Dad,

I am really glad that we have found each other.

Thanks for coming home and letting me meet you.

I hope that you have come to love me

as much as I have come to love you

in these few weeks we have known each other.

I am so glad that you are my dad.

Sleep well.

Love, your son, Ron."

I just sat there shaking my head and thinking, this young man is so vulnerable, so willing to open up his heart and express his love for a man he barely knows, especially one who abandoned him. What awesome qualities have been instilled in him by my own parents! He is truly a man of integrity. I am really proud that he is my son, even if it took me twenty five years to admit it.

"Love accomplishes miracles, doesn't it?"

"Yes," I said as several tears dropped on the note that I held in my lap. "It sure does!"

I had to see him to tell him I love him.

I knocked on Ron's door. "Ron, are you asleep yet?" There was no answer. "Ron." I knocked again. Still no answer, so I opened the door and saw him laying across his bed, still in his clothes, with no movement.

I rushed to him and called out his name again. "Ron, are you alright." It was obvious that something was radically wrong. His breathing was very shallow and his face was pale. I felt his pulse and it was barely detectable.

It seemed like an eternity of waiting, but Nine Eleven was there within a very few minutes and the paramedics went to work immediately to resuscitate him. They put an IV in his arm, put him on a gurney, rushed him to the ambulance and with sirens blaring raced for the hospital. I was right behind them.

While they were working on Ron at the condo, I had called Dr. O'dell. He said he would meet us at the hospital. He was there by the time we arrived.

Ron was rushed into the Emergency Room and the medical staff, who had already been notified, were prepared to do all that could be done to save Ron's life. He was in critical condition, whatever it was.

I waited in the Emergency waiting room, pacing at first, but finally dropping into a chair. My heart was racing – and aching. Did I remember even how to pray? I prayed when I was a kid, but stopped when I left to do my own thing. It seems that I even ran away from praying.

I knew the "now I lay me down to sleep," prayer, but that didn't seem appropriate on this occasion, except maybe for the part that went, "If I should die before I wake…. O Jesus, that can't happen, not with Ron. We just got to know each other. Please let us have some more time together. I want to tell him the same thing that he told me in his note."

I don't know if that was a prayer or not. I just had to say something to someone.

"It was most certainly a prayer. And what's more, it was heard."

"Oh, thank you!" That's all I could think to say to whoever.

Dr. O'dell walked over and sat down in a chair beside me. "Lee, we have done all that we can to get Ron stabilized. He is breathing easier, his pulse is gaining, his vital signs are improving, but he has a long way to go to be out of the woods."

"What do you mean, Dr.?" I asked. "What is wrong? I thought he was just having trouble with his hip."

"Lee, when we ran all the tests to determine whether it is feasible to do a hip replacement, we discovered some other things that have developed that should have been corrected a long time ago. Ron has a major staph infection running through his system that has impacted his entire body. It has become sepsis. His temperature is very high and his blood system is contaminated. We did catch it before he went into septic shock.

It is not cancerous, but it is serious enough to be life-threatening. I am amazed that he has made it this far."

"Morgan," I said, "Ron told me earlier today that you wanted to talk with me about something. Was this it? Did he know about this following your private consultation with him?"

"Yes, he did. I told him what were the results of the tests, but he wanted me to talk with you and give you the particulars. He felt you should know and that you should hear it from me. We're going to admit him to the critical care unit of the hospital and do the best we can to control the infection. Our success in doing that will determine whether we will be able to plan on a hip replacement later on."

"When can I see him, Dr.?" I asked.

"The staff is getting him cleaned up from the work they had to do on him so you will be able to see him soon. Just remember, he has been through a lot and may not look as good as you would like for him to look. Also he may not be as responsive since he has been placed on a ventilator and given several shots to help get his body back in balance."

"From the way it sounds," I said, "the hip replacement seems to be the least important thing to consider. Is that right?"

"Yes, it is," Morgan replied. "Right now we need to do everything we can do to just keep him alive. We will do all we can with our medical knowhow. However, if you are in the habit of praying, you might do some of that also."

He left to go back in to Ron.

I had to talk with someone. I called Nora. She was the only one I could think of to call.

When I told her about Ron, she expressed her sorrow over what he was going through. She said that she had always liked him and really came to know him when he visited with mom at the nursing home. He came virtually every day and sat with her for a couple of hours each time, usually reading something to her, even though she could barely respond to what he was reading or saying.

It was good to hear Nora's voice and also to hear her say the good things she was saying about Ron. It served to give even more insight into the kind of son I had and also served to remind me once again of how much I had missed by running away.

Nora commented that Ben and others had been inquiring about Ron and me and if anyone had heard anything from us since we arrived back in Portland. She suggested that I might want to call Ben and let him know what is happening.

I did that, but not before I told Nora how much I missed her and how I wished that Ron could have a nurse like her beside him now to see him through the tough times that he would be facing in the weeks and months ahead. We would most likely be in Portland for a very long time.

After talking with Nora, I called Ben. He thanked me for calling and giving him the details about Ron. He said he would notify all of his friends and also the Rev. Reinfeld, who thinks "an awful lot of Ron."

Everyone in Pryor thinks an awful lot of Ron. He has a whole town that will be thinking of him, and praying for him. I can use all the help in that area that I can get.

"Mr. Edwards," a nurse spoke from the door of the waiting room "you may now come in to see Ron. Please limit your stay to about fifteen minutes.

I followed her to Room 14 in the Emergency Ward. As I entered and walked to Ron's bedside I looked down on the near lifeless body of the young man that I had come to love so much in these past few weeks. He was so very pale and helpless..

"Ron," I said in a somewhat subdued voice, "I want you to know that I love you and I am so glad to have learned that you are my son. Thank you for the note you left on my pillow at the condo. I will never be able to fully tell you what that means to me. Ron, you're going to be alright. We'll both just hold on to the faith that mom talked to both of us about and, like she said, it will be okay." Inwardly, in my heart. I was sure hoping so.

He was not aware of my presence. I stayed for a few more minutes, just looking at him, and then went back to the waiting room. I was able to go back in his room for about fifteen minutes every three hours. Those were very long three hour periods and the fifteen minutes were so very short. The sleepless night passed very slowly.

Sometime in the night a nurse tapped me on the shoulder and awakened me to let me know that Ron had been moved to a room in the Critical Care Wing of the hospital. She asked me to follow her. It took awhile to straighten up my body from the cramped position in the wooden chair in which I had dozed off.

We made our way though the hallways of the hospital to what looked like a relative new section with private rooms and a nursing team for each room. We arrived at Room 120 that was very near the nurses' station where, I was told, he would be under closer observation.

Where had I known that room number before and heard that it was for the same reason? Mom! Mary-Martha! "O God, please don't let it turn out the same way!"

I sat in a very comfortable overstuffed chair near to Ron's bedside where I could rest comfortably and still be in close proximity in case he were to move or endeavor to speak. The nurse instructed me that the chair also lets down into a flat bed on which I could rest if I desired. She provided a blanket.

Ron was still very much under sedation, but appearing to be resting and sleeping more easily. Watching the rhythmic move of his chest up and down had its effect on me and I dozed off once again, only this time in a more comfortable position.

I awoke as a nurse gently touched me on the shoulder. I noticed that someone had been kind enough to place the blanket over me.

"Mr. Edwards, you have a phone call at the nurses' station. Would you like to take it in here or out there?"

"I will take it out at the nurses' station as I do not want to disturb his rest," I answered.

"Hello. Who is this? Marie, how on earth did you ever find me here at the hospital? We came in shortly after you left last night and I didn't even think about calling you.'

"I called for you this morning and the manager said that you took Ron to the hospital."

"Yes, the manager does keep an eye on what happens. I'm glad that you were able to get in touch with me. What's happening? Why did you call?"

"First, I called to see how you two are doing," she said. "How's Ron?"

"How's Ron? Well, Ron is very, very ill and right now is fighting for his life."

""Lee, I'm sorry to hear that," she said. He seems like a very fine young man and I enjoyed talking with him.

"Thank you for your kind words, Marie

"Lee, I'm also calling because the Rosses want to talk about their original offer on the condo."

"They want to talk about the condo? Marie, I'm not sure I want to get involved with them again. I really do appreciate all your work and the efforts you have made to get this settled, but after our "encounter" yesterday I'm not sure I'm up to their bickering and haggling again, especially right now with Ron so seriously ill. I now have other, more important things on which I want to spend my energies.

"Do I have your permission to go ahead and talk with them about it?" she asked.

"Yeah, Marie, why don't you go ahead and talk with them then let me know if they are willing to stick with their original agreement. Also let them know that the condo comes "as is" with nothing to be fixed up or repaired or replaced or repainted or re-anything. It is either taken as it is or it isn't taken at all. I'll find another buyer. Okay? Okay. You can reach me here at the hospital for this is where I will be staying until I am sure that Ron is out of the woods. Bye."

I couldn't help but think that the Rosses were partly responsible for Ron being where he is now. Had they done what they agreed to in the first place he would not have told them off and spent his energies declaring what he thought about people who lack integrity.

Come to think of it, I should have been the one telling them off and what I think about people who lack integrity. Well, at least telling them off. Who am I to say anything about anyone who lacks integrity? I need some work in that area myself.

Days passed slowly and little by little Ron regained energy – partly via the steak and potatoes administered through the IV tube, but mostly through his dynamic will to live. He also had a superior team of nurses that were careful to follow every detail required in helping his body to fight off the poisons within his system. Morgan O'dell was a worker of miracles.

Time was slipping by and I knew that I had to find another place to live.

I called Marie to find out if the Rosses had decided anything. She said that they had decided to go with their original agreement and so closing papers would be signed within the week. Then I knew that I really did have to seriously give search for a new place.

However, Marie also told me that once she told the Rosses about Ron's situation and my involvement with him, they said they could wait for another month before taking possession of the condo, if that was alright with me. And too, would I be willing to pay rent for that month? They wanted to be fair. Why not? Let's be fair. I'll pay the rent. At least I had a place to live for another month.

Two weeks passed before Ron was able to communicate. The intubation and the ventilator had affected his vocal chords so every effort at forming words was met with resistance. Ultimately, though, sounds began to form and he began to put whole sentences together, then whole paragraphs, then it was virtually impossible to get him to take a breath so that I could say something.

Two more weeks passed and during that time Ron began to sit up in bed, eat Jell-O and drink 7Up, the all-American healing medicines. Color began to return to his face and body, the antibodies were doing their work clearing the poison from his system and little by little he – and I, began to believe that he was, in fact, going to live.

I had called Nora, Ben and some others, including Ted at the farm to tell them that plans were beginning to be made for Ron to be moved to a rehabilitation center where he could get physical and occupational therapy. That would be happening within another week or so. Ted agreed to stay on at the farm as long as necessary.

By this time Marie had helped me find another apartment in which to move my personal belongings from the condo. It was close to the rehabilitation center to which Ron would soon be going. She also handed me a sizeable check at the closing for the condo. It would be needed to help pay the expenses related to Ron's medical bills.

One day as I walked out of his room into the hall thinking about all the things that had been happening over the past two months or so and especially that Ron was alive, I simply said, "Oh thank you God."

"You're welcome!"

"You did hear!"

I just leaned with my back against the wall, slide down until I was sitting on the floor, put my head on my arms and knees and began to cry. And cry! And cry!

"Lee."

I looked up through tear-filled eyes and there stood Nora. "Nora!" I jumped to my feet, grabbed her in my arms and swung her around in the hallway. "Oh God, it's so good to see you. What in the world are you doing here? What about your job? When did you get here? How did you get here? Where are you staying? How long can you stay?"

"Lee, put me down," she said. "Put me down! What will people think?"

"Oh, gosh Nora, I'm sorry. No. I'm not sorry. I'm so glad to see you. I really don't care what anyone would think." I burst into tears all over again. I thought my heart would jump right out of my chest. All I could do was stand and stare at her with tears running down my face.

She didn't seem to mind when I grabbed for my handkerchief and blew my nose. It was loud and sounded like one of the fog horns on the lobster trawlers.

"Lee," she said, accompanied by her captivatingly beautiful smile, "in one of your earlier phone calls – the first one I think, you said that you wished that Ron could have a nurse like me to take care of him through the tough times he would be facing. Well, I'm here. I'm here for the tough times. I'm here to do just that. I took an extended leave of absence from the staff at the nursing home.

"I've decided that I'm going to be here for Ron and you during the tough times ahead until he gets back on his feet. I know how to do nursing and you don't. You do what you have to do and I will do what I know how to do and it will all be okay. I'll stay as long as you need me."

"*How long do you need her, Lee? What does your heart say?*"

"F-O-R-E-V-E-R!" I yelled in a very loud voice that echoed down the hospital hallways.

Nora and I just stood there and looked at each other. I wanted to grab her and squeeze her as hard as I could.

"*Well?*"

"Well, what? Oh!" So I grabbed her and squeezed her as hard as I could.

CHAPTER 26

I rented another room in the apartment complex in which Marie had gotten me a room so that Nora would also have a place to stay while in Portland. I wanted her to be close so that we could have dinner together on a regular basis, which amounted to almost every evening following her work with Ron. Since I insisted - no, since I *suggested* that we have dinner together on a regular basis, I committed myself to be the one to pay the check.

After the staff at the Rehabilitation Center saw her credentials, they were very happy to have her come on board to help with his rehabilitation. She spent time every day working to help him walk again and to encourage him in both his physical therapy and counseling sessions. He had been through a lot and needed to talk through a lot of things that were hanging heavy on his mind - including issues related to his newly-found father.

Time passed more quickly with Nora there and also being able see the good progress that Ron was making. Sometimes all I could do was stand and look at the two of them as they went through the routines that served to restore life and health to this, my son. I could see that it was a struggle for him, but I also saw in him a determination to accomplish a level of health and vigor that would get him prepared for yet another major physical challenge – the replacement of a shattered hip. But that would have to come later.

It was evening and Nora and I had just said 'goodnight' to each other as we parted and went to our separate apartments. As I entered my door, the phone was ringing. I picked it up to hear Ben's voice, calling from Pryor.

"Hello Ben." I said. "It is good to hear your voice."

"It's good to hear you, also," he said. "Is Ron doing okay, and how is Nora? We miss her around here."

Yes!" I said. "Ron is doing great and Nora is certainly a Godsend. Her coming has worked something of a miracle in both our lives."

"Good. I'm glad to hear that," he said. I also wanted to let you know how things are going with Ted at the farm. I have been keeping in touch with him on a fairly regular basis and he stops in at the store once in awhile. Things at the farm are in great shape."

"Thank you, Ben," I responded. "I really do appreciate you keeping in touch with him. I know he appreciates it."

"You've been gone quite a long time, Lee, he said. "Are you sure everything is alright?"

"Yes," I said, "we have been gone a long time. Almost three months. We will all be glad when it's over and we can return home."

"Home! It sounds good, doesn't it?"

"It sure does." I said aloud.

"What did you say, Lee?" Ben asked.

"Oh, Ben," I said, "I was just talking to myself."

"Lee," he said, "you've got to quit doing that you might start answering yourself and then you could get in real trouble."

"Yeah, I know," I replied. "It's become quite a habit lately.

"Lee, I also wanted to let you know about the insurance company and what they plan to do with Clint."

"The Insurance Company? I had almost forgotten about that whole matter. What about it?

"They are going to take Clint to court, to recoup some of the losses they had through the embezzlement? "

"When do they plan to do this?"

"The preliminary hearing is next week, on Wednesday."

"Wow, Ben, I suppose they will want Ron and me there, but they haven't contacted us yet about it. If they do I'll have to figure out a way to come back by myself because Ron isn't ready to travel yet. He's gaining daily but still fragile and has lost a lot of weight. He's still in rehabilitation and counseling.

"Ben, you've been a part of mom and dad's business for years. Would you be willing to represent the Edwards family's interest in the case? You have the legal knowhow and also have audited their books on a regular basis and you are the one who discovered what was happening with Clint at the Feed Store.

"I can do that, Lee. The insurance company has already contacted me about it."

"Oh, they've already contacted you? Good. I will make every effort to be there by the time of the preliminary hearing. I'll ask Nora if she will be willing to stay on here with Ron.

"Thanks for calling, Ben. I really appreciate you and all that you have done and are doing to help out what's left of the Edwards family. Goodnight!"

"Good night, Lee," he said, as the conversation was ended.

With that I began to prepare for bed, while at the same time thinking I should let Nora know about my conversation with Ben.

That can wait until tomorrow!

Just as I was dropping off to sleep the phone rang again. "Hello. Oh, hi Morgan. What's up?

"Lee, I know it's late, but I think I need to come over and talk with you about Ron?"

"Ron? What about him? Is he okay?

"He' okay. Is it alright to come over?"

"Sure you can come over and talk with me about him. I'll wait up."

"Are you at the Honaker Drive address?"

"That's right, 2212 Honaker Drive, Apartment 12. And, Oh, Morgan, should we have Nora in on the conversation?

"I think that would be a good idea," he answered.

"Okay, I'll see if she is still up. She has an apartment right across the hall. See you in a few."

I could not help but wonder what that was all about; that he should take the time to come by my place to talk about Ron so late at night.

I got up, got dressed and then knocked on Nora's door to see if she was still awake. "Nora, are you still up? I'm sorry to be disturbing you so late."

She came and spoke to me through the closed door.

"Yes, Lee, I'm still awake. I was just laying in bed reading a book. What is it you want?"

"Dr. Odell just called and wants to come over and talk about Ron. He thought it might be a good idea for you to be in on the conversation."

"Okay. I'll put something on and be over in a few minutes."

"Thanks Nora. I really appreciate it."

Dr. O'dell arrived in about half an hour and thanked us for being available to talk with him about Ron. Come to find out, he was leaving town for a couple of weeks, beginning early tomorrow morning, and felt it important to talk about Ron's progress and proposed treatment before he left.

"Ron is doing fine," he said. "I am truly amazed at how that young man has recovered from such a serious infection throughout his system. Medicine has helped some, but he has a will and a faith that is really strong and both have played a major part in the recovery.

Morgan continued, "I have talked with the medical team, all except for Nora – and I'm glad you're here Nora, and we think that within about ten days Ron should be able to travel back home. In the meantime, I have checked with the Robert's Medical Center in Memphis, that is nearer to you, and they also have an excellent rehabilitation program that will serve Ron very well from here on out.

"And too, when he has fully recovered from this bout of illness, that same Center has a doctor friend of mine on its staff that is an expert in hip replacement surgery. In fact, that is all he does, replace hips. He decided to specialize in that while we were still in medical school together. I should have suggested it to you before, Lee, but you seemed determined that I should be the one to examine Ron.

"I'm glad you did because our hospital is probably better equipped to deal with the kind of infection that Ron has experienced. Maybe you were led by some inner sense to insist that he be brought here!"

"Yes," I said. "Maybe it was some inner sense that directed me to do it."

"Yes, it was some inner sense that directed you to do it," echoed the voice from somewhere inside me.

"Morgan and Nora," I said, "I received a phone call when I returned to my apartment awhile ago. It was from Ben Robertson in Pryor letting me know that Clint Burdett was being extradited and brought to court for a hearing regarding an embezzlement charge brought against him by my parents - who are now deceased, and the insurance company. That hearing is to be held next Wednesday in Pryor. Ben asked if I would be able to be there."

"Of course you will," said Nora. "I will be here with Ron. You can take a flight, be there for the hearing and then come back for when it's time to take Ron back home. That's settled.

"Dr. O'dell, he doesn't need to be here for anything regarding Ron between now and then, does he?" She asked.

"No," he said. Nothing I can think of. You and the staff have everything pretty well under control.

"You do what you have to do, Lee, and the staff will take care of Ron." Dr. O'dell said, "I'm only sorry that I have to be gone for the two weeks, but it's a medical convention and I need to be there. I've already talked with Ron about it and he feels like he's in good hands with Nora and the rest of the staff."

"Okay," I said, that's settled. I'll make arrangements tonight for the flight and if I can get one for tomorrow, I'll stop by and visit with Ron before I leave."

With that, Morgan said goodnight and excused himself and said he would be in touch with me later when he returned from the convention.

Nora and I stood in the doorway of the apartment and watched as he walked down the hall, out of the building and to his car.

I turned and looked at Nora. I could not help but notice how beautiful she was even without makeup, with her hair in disarray, her body wrapped in a loose fitting robe, with fuzzy slippers on her feet and that disarming smile that showed beautiful white teeth that seemed always to be framed by her desirable lips. I couldn't take my eyes off her.

"She's very special, isn't she?"

"Oh, yes," I thought.

"And she's also the kind of person you would want to have respect for you, right?"

"Oh, yes," I thought.

"Then why don't you just tell her goodnight and that you will see her tomorrow morning."

'Nora," I said, "Thank you very much for being here. You are really a special woman. I look at you and….Nora, goodnight. I will see you tomorrow morning."

She grinned at me, gave me a hug, kissed me on the cheek and returned to her own apartment. I closed the door and wondered if I could even make it to my bed. I thought I was going to have cardiac arrest.

.

CHAPTER 27

The court hearing was held in the county courthouse with honorable Judge Timothy Lawyer presiding. I couldn't help but wonder if his parent's family name had anything to do with the profession he chose. He had been judge in the county for a number of years and was highly respected by the citizens he served. I learned from Ben that he was known for his integrity, his fairness, his desire for justice to be served and his strict adherence to the law. He was also known to be considerate towards everyone who took the stand in his courtroom

It felt kind of good to be back in a courtroom again. However, this was different from the city setting in which I had participated with the firm in Portland. Here I found my faith renewed in the justice system.

I looked around and the court room was packed with people who lived in and around Pryor. Some were there in support of the Burdett family, others were curious and a few looked like they were angry.

I discovered that in this more rural setting, each person was addressed with politeness and respect. Even Clint was not treated as a crook, but as a local citizen who had made some bad choices.

When he was escorted into the court room he was politely greeted by Judge Lawyer, "Good morning, Mr. Burdett. It has been a long time since I have seen you. I remember when you used to play on the high school football team. You were a really good running back. Now we're going to find out what has been happening in your life since you graduated and went off to college."

Wow! I thought, that wasn't exactly how I had been thinking that an embezzler should be treated. Throw the book at him, judge. That would have been the way they did it in the city. I found myself taking copious notes as both attorneys spoke. I used to do that when I worked for the law firm in Portland – the one that fired me, I remembered.

The court stenographer was kept busy taking verbatim statements.

The Insurance Company attorney, a Mr. George Smyth – spelled with a "y" the court stenographer was reminded, presented the case against Clint. He did it in a way that laid out the facts as they were known, clearly, simply and with no accusatory tone in his voice. He was from one of the larger cities in the state, but evidently he had heard about Judge Lawyer, or the Judge had spoken to him personally about what was and was not allowed in his courtroom.

Clint had hired an attorney who practiced in the city in which he had been arrested. He presented a good case on Clint's behalf, even though it became evident from early on that he was guilty of the embezzlement charge.

When both attorneys finished presenting their opening statements, testimony was heard. Mr. Smyth put Ben on the stand in order to ask him to present the information of which he was aware regarding my folk's business, the auditing of the books and answer whatever other questions the attorneys might have to ask.

When Ben stepped up to the witness stand, the Judge greeted him, "Good morning, Ben. It is good to see you again. It's been awhile since you have stood before the Bench. How are things going at the store?"

"They're just fine, Your Honor. Thank you for asking." Ben replied.

Ben was sworn to tell the truth, the whole truth and nothing but the truth, so help him God. He was a man of integrity and truth was a given for him, at least the Ben I had come to know in the past few months, so it would not be difficult for him to answer in the affirmative.

He answered the questions asked by both attorneys. When he spoke of what had happened at the Feed and Seed Store, he related about the request by my parents to have the store books audited and in the process of auditing found a major discrepancy in the way the books were kept.

Having a law degree and having practiced law himself, he was able to pretty well anticipate the kinds of questions that he would be asked and he had a ready answer each time, evidently to the satisfaction of the questioning attorneys and also for Judge Lawyer.

Knowing the seriousness of the charges against Clint, and what he had done to decimate my parents income, the tone of Ben's voice never once, as far as I could determine, belittled Clint or made him out to be the worst criminal around.

I was not asked to take the stand or give any testimony. Ben had made an adequate statement relative to what the situation was and there was nothing of importance that I could have added.

However, as Ben stepped down from the witness stand, Judge Lawyer did ask him about Ron. "Ben, where is Ron Edwards? Was he not asked to be present for the hearing, since he was involved in bringing the charges?"

"Yes, your Honor," Ben answered. "He would have been here if he could. He has been in Portland for the last couple of months, hospitalized with a very serious illness related to a crushed hip, staph infection and other complications as a result of an automobile collision five years ago that crushed his hip."

"I'm sorry to hear that," Judge Lawyer said. "Was that the accident in which CJ was killed?

"Yes, your Honor,"

"And what was the outcome of that accident? I was not involved in that case. It was investigated, I presume?"

"Yes, your honor, it was investigated. The County Sheriff's conclusion was that it was caused by a hit and run drunk driver. That person has never been found."

"Has Ron been taking care of the farm since CJ's death?" Judge asked.

"Yes, your honor," Ben replied, "but he was badly crippled in the accident and that was the main reason he went to Portland, to talk about possible hip replacement. Since arriving there it has been discovered that he has far more serious things to think about, like staph infection. He is confined to a rehabilitation center and that is why he couldn't be here today."

Throughout his testimony Ben had said nothing about the suspicions and conclusions that some of the citizens had come to regarding the accident or that the Sheriff had been notified of those conclusions or that he was not voted back into office at the next election or that he, like his nephew, had disappeared from the county and state.

"Give our best regards to Ron when you see him," said Judge Lawyer. "I am sorry for his misfortune."

"I will do that, your Honor. Thank you."

"Thank you, Ben," said Judge Lawyer. Then looking toward the attorneys' tables he said, "Let's continue with the case at hand."

Clint's parents were also present in the courtroom. They had come to support their son as he was going through the ordeal of having charges filed against him for embezzlement.

When Mr. Burdett was placed on the witness stand, Judge Lawyer greeted him, "Good morning Ralph. How are things going out at the farm?"

"Pretty well, your Honor, except we're having a little trouble getting help right now."

"I'm truly sorry to hear that." Judge replied. "I hope things get better for you."

When Mr. Burdett began answering the attorneys' questions, he said that he simply could not believe that Clint had done what he was accused of doing. He had always been a fine boy and young man. He had worked hard to make something of himself. They were proud of the fact that he went to college and earned an Associate's Degree in Business Administration.

"Mr. Burdett," asked the attorney, "Have you been in touch with Clint since he left Pryor?"

"Yes," he said. "We have been in touch with Clint since he left town a few years back. And, we believe him when he said he wanted to quit working at the Feed Store and work in another place doing something else. Other young people had left Pryor for the same reason."

I could identify with that. Wasn't that the reason I left? I didn't want to work the farm and stay in Pryor the rest of my life. At least that is the reason I remember using for my exit.

"Mr. Burdett," the attorney asked, "your son is accused of the embezzling of funds from the Edward's Feed and Seed Store. Do you believe the accusations to be true?"

'No,' he replied, "we believe our son, Clint, is innocent of the things that are being said about him and feel that the Burdett name has been maligned by those accusing our son of embezzlement. We feel that the business lost money because local farmers were buying their feed and seed at a larger store in the nearby city and at a cheaper price."

"How long have you and your son lived in Pryor?" asked the attorney.

He answered, "We have been residents in Pryor a long time. Clint has grown up in Pryor, went through the Pryor schools and was away from town only when he attended college in another city."

Ralph Burdett answered the questions as best he could, all the while he must have known in his heart that their son, Clint, had actually done what he had been accused of doing. Yet they were loving parents and wanted to be there for their son. Even as Mr. Burdett answered the various questions, both parents kept their eyes focused on Clint. Mrs. Burdett spent much of the morning wiping tears from her eyes.

When Mr. Burdett had finished his testimony, Judge Lawyer said, "Thank you, Ralph, for your testimony. I know that it is a difficult thing for a parent to do, but it is necessary so that we can come to know the truth in this matter and justice can be served for everyone."

When all the questions had been asked and answered, the decision handed down by Judge Lawyer was that enough evidence had been presented that there would be a trial. He set the date with which both attorneys agreed and court was dismissed.

The Burdetts were allowed by Judge Lawyer to embrace and weep with their son, Clint, before he was to be removed from the courtroom and placed once again in the county jail.

I couldn't help but look on the brokenness of this family who had been an integral part of the Pryor community for years. I grew up with Clint. We went through school together. I had left town about the time he went away to college. We were never close friends because we ran in different circles, but we were never enemies either.

I think Clint was aware of my presence in the courtroom throughout the morning, but never once, to my knowledge, did he make eye contact with me. I found myself wishing that he had so that I could let him see that I had forgiven him. I realized that I did not have one feeling of anger or bitterness in my heart toward him.

I felt sorry for his parents. I could not imagine what must be happening inside the broken hearts of these two ordinary people who loved their son in an extraordinary way. I couldn't help but wonder if my parents had shown their love for me to others in the same way, even though I had run away and never bothered to contact them.

There was no desire in me, whatsoever, for vengeance or retribution against this family, only sorrow for what they would be facing in the future. Little did I know at the time what they would be facing!

In a community the size of Pryor, back then - and even now, there was a community spirit. Whether or not you related to the same crowd you were still a part of the community. You may have your community quarrels and family skirmishes, but let someone from the outside criticize you or speak against your school, or farming practices – or anything else for that matter, and suddenly everyone stood together, back to back, like the musk ox protecting its young against the marauding wolf pack.

Yes, I knew Clint to be guilty of the embezzlement and he would have to suffer the consequences for what he did, but I no longer hated him for what he did. At one time I had even vowed to break his neck if ever I had the opportunity. Something had totally removed that from me.

Then came the shocker!

.

CHAPTER 28

As the proceedings wrapped up for the day and as Clint was being escorted toward the exit for a return to his cell, he turned toward Judge Lawyer and spoke for the first time. "Your Honor," he said, "may I speak to the court? And may I speak for the record?"

Judge Lawyer had already started to exit from the bench, but when Clint spoke to him he turned around and said, "Yes, Clint. You may speak, but have you consulted with your attorney about what you want to say?"

"No sir," Clint said, "I have not talked with him, but I need to say something that I feel is very important and can save you and the people here a lot of trouble. I think it can also save the county a lot of expense."

Judge Lawyer stepped back up to the bench and sat down. He tapped the gavel on the desk and called the court back into session. All those who had been standing and ready to exit the court room, turned around and found their seats once again.

"This is a little unusual," he said, "but I want to give Mr. Burdett opportunity to address the court, and it will be recorded as a part of this court's proceedings."

The court stenographer quit putting her equipment away and proceeded to get it ready once again to record everything that was to be said. As soon as she was ready, Judge Lawyer said, "Go ahead Clint."

"Thank you, your Honor." Clint began, "I owe a lot to my parents and the people of Pryor for the way all of you helped me through school, cheered me on when I was on the football team, voted me the one in high school most likely to succeed, encouraged me when I went away to college, congratulated me when I came home with a degree in Business Administration and told me what a great job I was doing in helping out Mr. & Mrs. Edwards by running their store for them.

"I could not have asked for better parents and for any better support than what I have received from this community in my youth and young adult years. I was so proud to have a place here. Pryor was home to me. I was really happy to return home from college and take up residency here.

"Then, when I began to work at the Edwards' store I was even more proud because they trusted me to run the store for them and handle the money and the books. Mr. Robertson can tell you that things went real well for quite a few years because he and Charlie Higgins always audited the books and every year they balanced out to the penny. Didn't they, Mr. Robertson?"

I noticed him looking straight into the face of Ben and I also noticed Ben nodding his head in agreement as he looked back at Clint.

"Yes, son, they did."

"I was doing pretty good. Mr. and Mrs. Edwards paid me good wages and I saved and bought me the kind of pickup truck I always wanted, one with big wheels and double steel bumpers. I think I was the only one in the county that had a truck like that one. I worked hard to save money in order to buy it. It took awhile, but I bought it.

"Your Honor, I am not trying to blame anyone else for the horrible choice I made. I accept full responsibility. However, one day my Uncle Jerry, who was County Sheriff at the time, stopped by the store. And as we were talking he suggested that I might want to make a little more money off the store by working the books myself. After all, he said, I had a Business Administration Degree and that should qualify me to keep the books and audit them myself. He suggested that in doing so I could make a few changes in the records so that I could have more income.

"After all," Uncle Jerry told me, "you probably could use some extra income to help pay for that truck you bought."

"I knew it was wrong and I felt awful doing it, but I followed his suggestion and began taking money and working the books to cover it up. The store had the same kind of business as before but showed less and less profit.

"When Mr. and Mrs. Edwards insisted that they have the books audited by Mr. Robertson I knew he would find out what had been happening. He would know immediately that I had been taking money from the store proceeds.

"Judge Lawyer, I want this court to know, and I want the good people of Pryor to know, that I am guilty of the embezzlement for which I have been charged."

Audible gasping, mumbling and loud whispers - as well as crying, could be heard through the court room. There was not a lot of disturbance like the kind I had found in the city court rooms, but enough so that Judge Lawyer's gavel found the top of the desk and he said, just loudly enough to be heard, "That will be enough, friends. Continue, Mr. Burdett."

"Well, I became scared. Then I became angry and accused them of not trusting me. Words were exchanged and I stormed out of the store, hating what I had done, but also hating them. My anger took over and controlled me. The only thing I could think to do was to do something to take it out on them.

"So, when I felt the time was right, I had worked out a plan. I knew what I would do. First, I got drunk. I know now that if I hadn't gotten drunk I don't think I would have ever done what I did.

"I knew when Mr. Edwards and Ron were going out to deliver seed and groceries to a family in the country so I waited on a side road. When I saw his old pickup coming back in toward town I gunned my motor and rammed into its side. I saw that it was badly smashed and it looked like he and Ron were really hurt. I was even more scared, so I backed up and drove away as fast as I could, still mad, sorry for what I had done, but it was too late to undo it.

"I got in touch with Uncle Jerry as soon as I could and when I told him what had happened, he told me that he would take care of it, so not to worry about it. He told me a place to go over in Fayetteville and stay with a friend of his. He gave me the address and phone number and said he would be in touch with them to tell them that I would be staying there for awhile. He would take care of any expenses related to it. I was not to tell anyone about what had happened. I went to Fayetteville, like he told me, and kept quiet.

"I was not aware at the time that Mr. Edwards had been killed in the collision and that Ron had his hip smashed. That was not my intention. I'm not sure what my intention was, but I know it was not to cause Mr. Edwards' death or cripple Ron. I was also not aware, until later, that Uncle Jerry blamed the hit and run accident on an unknown drunk driver. At least that part he told about was true.

"I am truly sorry for the grief I have caused my mom and dad, my friends in Pryor and the Edwards family in particular. I simply cannot live with myself any longer. Neither can I continue blaming Uncle Jerry for my bad decisions and trying to not accept the responsibility for what I have done.

"Thank you, your Honor, for allowing me to speak to the court. I had to do it. This has weighed heavy on my conscience all these years and somehow I just knew that today I had to confess it to you and everyone here. I do not ask you to excuse me for what I have done. I do pray that all of you may someday find it in your hearts to forgive me. Thank you."

There was stunned silence in the packed courtroom. To my knowledge, never before or since has a courtroom in that county experienced anything like it did today.

Judge Lawyer spoke, "Mr. Burdett, you did, indeed, listen to some very poor advice from someone you should have been able to trust to give you wise counsel. That does not excuse what you have done because you have in fact betrayed the very families and community that put their trust in you. And as a result you have brought a lot of suffering on both them and yourself.

"Nor," he continued, "does it excuse your uncle from complicity in both the embezzlement and possible cover up of the car crash. The court will look into that.

"Thank you for telling the truth. That is the only way that justice can be served, when we know the truth of what happened. I trust that your telling of what happened will also serve to bring some kind of peace to your own troubled spirit."

"Bailiff," the Judge said, "please return Mr. Burdett to his cell. Attorneys, I would like to visit with you in my chambers. We have some work to do. Court dismissed, and this time I mean it is dismissed." The gavel hit the desk, as Judge Lawyer sat for a moment looking at Clint's grieving parents embracing each other.

Ben and I just glanced at each other with a "suspicions confirmed" look, but also acknowledging a certain level of respect for a man who had enough of a conscience left to want to make an effort to right a terrible wrong, even if it might mean spending the rest of his life in prison.

"Remember, I said to you that your forgiveness of Clint may serve to set him free from his irresponsibility and become someone more than who he is?"

"Yes, I remember," I said half aloud.

"What was that you said?" Ben asked.

"Nothing," I replied. "I guess I was just talking to myself again and remembering something I said to myself awhile back."

As we walked out of the courtroom I could not help but express my feelings to Ben that I had actually witnessed a civil and civilized courtroom experience this morning, the likes of which I had never witnessed before.

He grinned and said, "Judge Lawyer will have it no other way. When he is in charge, everyone knows that they are in his world. He expects and demands civility.

"You could tell by the way he conducted today's session that he models what he expects from everyone else involved in a case. He approaches each person, regardless of what they have done or have been accused of doing, as a human being and he treats them humanely. If you indicate otherwise, attorney or not, you may find yourself setting in the hallway waiting for the session to be over while your client sits at the table all by their self."

I had already decided that I liked that Judge!

CHAPTER 29

As we walked away from the courthouse, Ben asked if I would like to have lunch with him at Tony's Café. He said that it was a good place to eat and they served very good lunches at a reasonable price. I told him, "Sure."

I had never eaten at Tony's, but the name rang a bell somehow. It was at the edge of town out on the highway and it seemed like a very popular place for truckers. Six or eight eighteen wheelers were parked in the large parking area at the back of the café.

It was then that I remembered where I had heard the name of the café before. Ben had mentioned to me that was where Ron's mother, Bonnie, worked while my folks took care of him. It was also the place where she met her future truck-driver husband, the one who didn't want Ron after they had a child of their own.

Ben and I sat in a booth located somewhat toward the back of the café. I sat on the side that faced the front door. What was it about the place that caused me to become anxious? I had no reason to be. It was just a café where she had worked some twenty of so years ago.

Nevertheless as I looked around the place I began to wonder if that was the same coffeemaker where she made coffee and served it to the truckers. Did she take the plates of food from that pass-through window that connected the kitchen to the front of the café and serve the people at this booth? Did she slide that glass door on the dessert cupboard to reach for a piece of lemon cream or apple pie to serve her truck-driver? Did she press the keys of that particular cash register when people stepped up to pay their bills? Did they give her a good enough tip to help pay her bills?

"Lee. Lee." Ben spoke to me and waved his hand in front of my face. He finally got through to me and I came back from wherever my mind had gone. I didn't feel a need to tell him where my mind had gone.

"Oh, sorry Ben," I said. "I was just looking around at the café. It seems like a pretty busy place."

"It really is," he said. "I eat here quite often because they always seem to have good food. Shorty, the cook, is very good at what he does."

"Shorty?" I asked.

"That's right, Shorty."

"We had a kid in Pryor that I went to school with that everyone called Shorty. Is that the same one?"

"The one and only."

"You know," I said, "it always seemed strange that a guy that was 6'6" would be called 'Shorty.' I could never figure that out."

"Neither could anyone else," he said, "but it stuck. And now he's about 6'9" and apparently going for 7' from the looks of it. Think of it, forty years old and almost seven feet tall. A sure stand out in any crowd! Pardon the pun."

"As I remember, he was always good natured about it and never took offense at anyone for calling him that."

"He has a great attitude," Ben said. "And, he's a great cook."

The waitress brought our drinks and orders and we began to eat. No sooner had we begun than there was a commotion near the front of the café that created some kind of disturbance, not unpleasant, but noticeable.

There was fairly loud laughter with people greeting other people, male and female voices sounding like a reunion of some kind was taking place. Those who weren't talking were waving their hands at a fellow who had just entered the café.

"It's been a long time."

"Yeah, too long!"

"When did you get into town?"

"Just now."

"What took you so long?"

"Just happened to get a load that brought me back through Pryor."

"Well, it's good to see you. Where's the wife?"

"She's in the truck. She'll be in pretty soon."

"How're the kids? Are they with you?"

"No, the oldest one is grown and has a kid of his own. Danny stayed with my folks so that he could keep up with his classes in high school."

"They really grow up fast don't they?"

"Sure do."

I had to remember that it's kind of like that in smaller towns when people get together that haven't seen each other in quite a while. I also had to remember that in a town like this when people greet each other like that in a place like this, it becomes a community social. People are either waving at each other in recognition and welcome, or else eavesdropping, like me.

Ben was one of the wavers. He evidently recognized the trucker that had come into the café and who had gotten into conversation with others who were locals and asking all the questions.

Then came the surprise of all surprises, on this day of all days. She came through the front door of the café and everyone turned to look at her.

"Bonnie!" someone yelled out.

"Welcome, home girl. We miss you around here." Another voice chimed in.

"When are you going to leave this trucker and come back to the rest of us?" Still another voice tuned in to the conversation.

She just stood there smiling and waving at the ones who had become her friends during the years she worked at the café. Her trucker-husband walked over and put his arms around her, squeezed her up against him and said, "Sorry, guys, she's all mine and she wants it that way. And so do I." Then he kissed her on the side of her head.

She was gorgeous! At about forty two years of age she was still young and beautiful. Giving birth to three children had not had any bad effects on her figure. And riding around in an eighteen wheeler with her trucker-husband had not put any wrinkles on her face. She was beautiful – did I already say that? And she was obviously happy.

I just sat there, staring, when Ben said, "Well, I'll be, if it isn't Bonnie. Would you have believed that she would show up on this very day when you and I came here to eat?"

"Truthfully, Ben, I don't know what to believe. Nothing much surprises me anymore around this place. Seeing her brings back a lot of memories that I thought I had taken care of, but evidently need to do something more about. She's as beautiful now as when she was in high school. Maybe even more so!"

I didn't know whether or not I wanted her to see me, but there was no place to hide. The booth was kind of out of the way, but it wasn't invisible. I thought of going to the restroom, but noticed that the sign was past the cash register which would have necessitated going directly in front of her to get there. I cancelled that thought.

Since the booth wasn't invisible, maybe I could just pretend like I am. It didn't work.

Suddenly our eyes met and for the slightest period of time – maybe an hour, I don't know because time stood still, we looked at each other, both with disbelief written across our faces.

Then she smiled, walked over to our booth, greeted Ben and then reached out her hand as I began to stand up. Ben also stood up, gave her his seat and then walked into the cafe crowd. I guess he knew that Bonnie and I needed some private time.

In addition to everything else he does, and is, around Pryor, he certainly knows how to be sensitive to people who might find themselves in a possibly embarrassing situation.

Bonnie shook my hand and with a smile that lit up the room, said, "Lee. Lee Edwards. I cannot believe it. It is actually you, after all these years. You look as handsome now as you did when we were in high school together. Someone has taken really good care of you."

I think I blushed. At least it felt like it. My face was hot.

"Bonnie," I managed to speak her name after clearing my throat two or three times. Then I muttered something about what a surprise it was seeing her here in Pryor after all these years, but in my heart I wanted to cry out, "Bonnie, please forgive me for being such a jerk and doing what I did to you; for running away and leaving you to face everyone all by yourself; for never making any effort to help you with our son; for abandoning the two of you. Oh God, Bonnie, please forgive me."

The words were in my heart but they never found the exit sign to come out through my mouth.

"I'm glad we met, Lee," she said. I have been hoping for a long time that I would someday see you because there is something I have been wanting to say to you. And this is just as good a place to say it as any."

She looked around at the front of the café where her trucker-husband was in animated conversation with other trucker friends that he obviously had not seen in a long time, then she turned back to me.

"Lee, I know that what we did when we were kids was wrong. It should never have happened. But it did and I went to stay with an aunt and uncle over in Arkansas and gave birth to our son there. I named him Ronnie. Your folks kept him and raised him because my husband, who is standing right over there, did not want him after we had our first child. So in order to save my marriage and keep Ronnie from having a miserable life I took him back to your folks place. They agreed to raise him as their own. I think they already knew you were his father.

"I tried to keep in touch with him at various times, especially on his birthday and at Christmas, but soon discovered that in order for my marriage to work, that had to quit. Consequently, I never was able to see him grow up or know what was happening in his life. I felt like I was robbed two times – robbed of what I thought was my love for you and robbed of being able to watch our son grow up.

"The thing that I have been waiting to say to you if ever I got to see you is, Lee, I forgive you for doing what you did to me. I forgive you for being a jerk. I forgive you for running away and leaving me to face the pregnancy all by myself. I forgive you for never making an effort to help with Ronnie. I forgive you for abandoning the two of us."

I just sat there in disbelief. This woman had read my mind.

"And," she continued, "I've asked God to forgive me for the resentment that I held in my heart for you for several years. Your mom told me when Ronnie and I were staying with her that if I held on to my resentment it wouldn't hurt you, but it would kill me. It took me years to do it, but I did it and swore that if I ever saw you face to face I'd tell you. So here we are and I've said it."

"Bonnie, uh, uh, thank you," I stuttered. "I've been wanting for a long time to ask you to forgive me for the very things you spoke, but I didn't know if ever the opportunity would show up for it to happen. But it did. Even though you have told me already that you forgive me, I still need to ask you, "'will you forgive me?'"

"Yes!"

"Good. I knew that if I didn't ask you it would kill me, like mom warned. She got a lot of mileage out of that threat."

"Bonnie," I asked, "will there be an opportunity to tell you about Ron?"

"What do you know about Ron?" she asked.

"Well," I said, "I returned to Pryor about three or four months ago to find that my dad had been killed in a car accident about five years ago."

"Yes, I know. I had heard about that," she said. "He was a terrific man, though, as I remember, he was in alcohol rehabilitation most of the time Ronnie and I were at the farm."

"Well," I continued, "Did you know that Ron, who was about twenty at the time, was riding with him and the accident crushed his right hip and crippled him up pretty bad?

"No, I wasn't aware of that," she said. "It's been years since I have had any contact with your folks and Ronnie. How did you happen to meet him and come to know that he was your son? I never told anyone."

"When I came back to Pryor, after being gone for about twenty five years, I met Ron for the first time out at the farm. He has been taking care of it since dad's death, even though he is having difficulty walking. Right now he is in Portland in a physical therapy and rehabilitation center after fighting off a staph infection that just about took his life."

I quickly told her all that I could in the few minutes that we had about mom's death, the proposed hip replacement, what a fine young son she gave birth to and how highly thought of he is in Pryor. She would be proud of him.

All the while I really wanted to find a quiet place where she and I could sit down together and fill each other in on the details of our lives for the past twenty five years.

That was not to be. Her trucker husband called her name and told her it was time to haul on down the road. She got up from where she was seated, said goodbye, turned and walked over to him and I heard him ask about the guy that she was talking to. I heard her say, "We went to high school together here in Pryor and were good friends at the time."

They walked out the door arm in arm and I have never seen her since. Perhaps someday they will travel through Pryor again and she can find out more about the son she never knew, the one I have come to love as much as life itself.

CHAPTER 30

I got up from the booth, paid the bill for the food and began to look for Ben. I walked outside to find him waiting by his car. He drove me back to the convenience store where I could pick up my car and drive on out to the farm. No words were exchanged during the short trip across town to the store. We just sat silently in the car for a few minutes.

I guess he could see that my thoughts were not to be invaded, interrupted or disturbed after having witnessed the conversation between Bonnie and me. Thoughts need time to find some semblance of normalcy after a meeting like that.

"That was a difficult time for you wasn't it?"

"Yes, it was," I thought

"It was a necessary time for both you and Bonnie, wasn't it?"

Again I thought, *"Yes, it was."*

"Are you glad it happened?"

"Yes, in a way I am, but who would have thought that it would happen in the way it did, after all these years and suddenly we both show up in this café at the same time?"

"Sometimes life is like that, isn't it? It's full of surprises that come in ways you would never expect. Usually you are aware of them only if you quit shutting yourself off from the possibility."

"What does that mean?" I thought to myself.

"Well, you could have refused to have lunch with Ben and even when you did agree you could have refused to go to Tony's Café as he suggested because of possible memories it would bring back.

"And too, when you saw Bonnie you could have chosen to not pay attention to her or let yourself take the opportunity to talk with her. In other words, you could have shut it out and looked on the whole thing as an interesting coincidence.

"But you didn't. You let yourself be vulnerable and as a result the surprise meeting turned into a time of healing and closure for both you and her. Don't you feel better?"

"As a matter of fact, yes, I really do." I said aloud.

"What's that?" asked Ben. "You really do what?"

"Oh," I looked at Ben a little sheepishly, "I really do feel better. I was telling myself that I really do feel better."

"Feel better than what? If I may ask," said Ben.

"Feel better than I did before Bonnie and I had our talk back there at Tony's Café. She appears to be an amazing woman. We were able to take care of something that had been hanging over our heads since we were in high school together. It's been a long time coming but both of us are better because of it."

"I don't want to be presumptuous," said Ben, "or assume too much, but if you will pardon me, the thing you talked about that had been hanging over your heads since high school had to do with the fact that you are Ron's parents, right?"

"How did you know that?" I asked as I looked at him in disbelief.

"Lee," said Ben, "everyone in Pryor knew that you were Ron's father from the very first. You were the only boy that Bonnie ever had anything to do with in school. She wouldn't even look at anyone else. The two of you were inseparable and everyone could see, if they weren't badly mistaken, that you would probably wind up getting married soon after you both graduated from high school.

"Trouble was, you just let your hormones get out of control and messed it up for both of you. You're not the first kids to let it happen and you won't be the last, but you can't go through the rest of your life beating yourselves over the head. Somewhere you have to put it to rest and get on with living the life you have left to live.

"From what I saw today at the café, both you and Bonnie have taken a major step toward doing just that. She seems to be happily married and maybe one day you will be too."

"Besides, look at the man that your son Ron has become. Even with all that he has gone through he has grown up to be a man of integrity and with a strong faith. No one in town has every looked down on him because of the fact that he was born to people who were not married. That wasn't his fault.

'The only people who have really missed out on the joy of knowing this young man as he grew up are you and the Shoemakers, Bonnie's parents. They never could forgive her and they never could handle the embarrassment brought on them by what happened. They finally quit the Pryor school system and transferred to another district over in Arkansas. They have chosen to separate themselves from their daughter and their grandson. That is their loss and I know it's killing them.

"I'm sorry to hear that they did that," I told him. "I'm sure they were hurt because of what happened, but it's too bad they and Ronnie have missed out on so much."

"You, on the other hand," Ben said, "have every opportunity in the world to share in this young man's adult life and enjoy each other for whatever years you may have remaining. My suggestion to you, if you will hear it, is, don't mess it up or it'll kill you."

"You spent a lot of time around my mom, didn't you?"

"As a matter of fact, yes I did. She had a lot of wisdom about some things and a possible solution for a lot of other things."

I climbed out of Ben's car and went over to get into my own. The drive out to the farm was a short one so I took my time and drove up some of the other country roads just to allow my mind time to assimilate at least some of the things that had happened in the last couple of hours.

What started out as simply a time to have lunch with Ben turned into a reliving of a major emotional event in my life. I looked into the face and eyes of a woman I once knew well when she was a girl, but only know about, now that she is a woman. Yet, she is the very one who gave birth to our child.

Then to have Ben tell me that everyone in the whole state knew that I was Ron's father long before I would acknowledge it, really revealed to me how much I had been living in denial. I had been burying the truth for years without having any inclination or desire to deal with it.

Well, I thought, that's all out in the open now and I don't have to live in denial anymore. I am who I am. I am Ron's father and I am very glad he's my son. I simply cannot run away from that!

When I walked into the farmhouse a red light was flashing on the phone. I pressed the message button and heard the sound of Nora's voice.

"Lee, when you get this message give me a call. It's now about 1:30 and I will be at the rehab center until about 4:00. It's important so hope I will be able to talk with you today. I think you know the number here, but just in case, here it is." Then she gave me the number for the center. I'm glad she did because I didn't know that I had it or remembered it.

It was about 3:30, so I called as quickly as I heard the message. "Just a minute," the voice said, "I'll go get her." I found myself tapping my fingers on the wall by the phone as I waited for them to find Nora. Was I anxious or nervous about something?

"Oh, hi Nora, is everything alright?

"Yes, Lee, everything is fine."

"Oh, thank goodness," I answered. "I guess I was a little anxious when you said to call right away."

"I called to let you know that Ron can be released to come home."

"What's that? Ron can be released to come home? When?

"I can bring him home next week."

"Next week?" I shouted. "Wow, that is sooner than Dr. O'dell thought. Are they sure he's well enough to do that?"

"Lee," she said, with a slight sound of impatience in her voice, "the staff and I have decided that he's well enough to come home. Can you handle that?"

"Well," I said, "if the staff thinks so it is certainly okay with me. I will make plans to fly back to bring both of you home."

"No, Lee, there's no need for you to fly back here to get us. We will make it home on our own. You stay there."

"What did you say Nora? Me to stay here and you drive Ron home? Nora, that's asking an awful lot. You have done more than enough for both of us by...

"Lee Edwards," she spoke slowly and distinctly, "I will be driving Ron home from Portland to Pryor. You stay there! Do you understand me?"

"Well, since you put it that way, I'm certainly not going to argue with *you*! When do you think you will be arriving?

"We will be arriving about this time next week. I will call to let you know for sure when arrangements have been made, okay?

"About this time next week? I repeated. "Okay. If you need anything let me know.

"Oh, by the way, Nora, since I won't be coming there to bring you and Ron back here, I had better give Marie a call and tell her to close out my apartment and that I'll take care of the expenses for both yours and mine. Okay?"

"Thanks, Lee. I love you. Bye."

"You're welcome. Bye. Love you, too."

What? What did she say? What did I say? "I love you." Did I really hear her say that? "I love you, too!" Did I really hear myself say that?"

"Sounds awfully good, doesn't it?"

"What?" I asked.

"To have someone say "I love you," and then be able to tell someone in return "I love you too. Feels good doesn't it?"

"Actually it sounds strange telling a grown woman that I love her. I'm not in the habit of doing that with the women I have known. Love was not a part of my relationship with them.

"It took me awhile to tell Ron that I love him, but he's my son. Nora's different!"

"Why should it be so different with her? You're a healthy, robust male and she is a beautiful, caring female. Isn't that how life has been put together? Isn't there something somewhere about the two becoming one? Just because you messed it up once – or twice, or even three times, you don't have to mess it up again."

"You're right," I said. "I don't have to mess it up again and I'm not going to."

I found that I was still holding on to the receiver of the phone while I was having this dialogue with myself. So I just pushed the button on the cradle, dialed the number that Nora had given me, looked at the clock – it was right on 4:00 o'clock. I hoped that she was still at the center.

"Hello. Nora? Nora, I love you."

"What did you say, Lee?"

"What did I say? I said I LOVE YOU."

I had to hold the receiver away from my ear as she yelled into the one she was holding in her hand, 'I LOVE YOU, TOO."

I found myself laughing, crying, whooping, jumping up and down, slapping myself on the thighs and, in the process, dropped the phone crashing to the floor.

When I picked it up she asked, "Lee, are you alright? Did you fall? Did you hurt yourself? It sounded like you crashed to the floor. Are you okay?"

"Oh, I'm fine, I'm really fine. I'm more than fine. I'm super fine. In fact, I'm the finest of the fine. I'm drunk, fine." She probably thought I had actually gotten drunk.

I didn't tell her that I felt like my heart went into cardiac arrest because it couldn't find enough room in my chest to beat a normal beat. So it just took off on its own and raced with the wind, taking my breath with it. I think I need a defibrillator.

"Nora. Are you still there?" I asked after I got control of myself.

"Yes, Lee, I'm still here."

"Me too! I'm really glad that you will be here next week. Are you sure you don't want me to come there and drive you and Ron home? I will be more than happy to do it.

"Lee Edwards!"

"Okay, I'll wait. Bye."

I walked out from the kitchen to the back porch of the house, looked out past the barn over the fields that were just beginning to show green from the newly sprouting seeds and yelled at the top of my voice, "I ..LOVE... YOU, ...NORA!" and it echoed everywhere, bouncing off the walls of the barn., the water in the lake, the moon!

My yelling even scared some of the chickens that were pecking around in the yard. One or two of them took off with a sudden release of clucking and with such a burst of speed that they lost some of their feathers in the process. Guess they don't understand how humans express their emotions.

Ted stuck his head out of the barn door and yelled, "Did you call for me, Mr. Edwards? Are you okay, Mr. Edwards?"

I had forgotten all about him being on the place.

"Yeah, Ted," I yelled back. "I'm fine. "I'm more than fine. I'm really fine. In fact, I'm finer than fine. I'm fine, fine, fine!"

I felt like jumping in the air and clicking my heels, but remembered that the ability to do that pretty much ended about the time I took a huge spill when I tried to do it upon graduation from college. It took me a long time to get over the bruises. No need going through that again. Besides I didn't want to be sporting bruises all over my body when Nora returned.

The week went by very slowly. I was really anxious to see Nora, and Ron, of course. I was a little concerned about the two of them making that long trip with him just getting out of rehabilitation. However, I have discovered that Nora is quite capable of taking care of herself and she also knew how to handle Ron's health issues so they should be alright. Nevertheless, I was concerned about their welfare. In reality I was anxious to see both of them again. Truthfully, I wanted to go to Portland and bring them home myself.

However, further thinking helped me remember how she responded the last time I suggested it. Not a good idea!

CHAPTER 31

I spent the week helping Ted around the farm. It felt good to feed the livestock and generally help doing the chores that are part of Farming 101: milk the cows, muck the stalls, feed the chickens, fill the water troughs and do the other little mundane things that keep the wheels turning. I hadn't done that since I ran away from the farm at eighteen.

It was easy to see that Ted was right at home, having grown up on his parent's farm just a few miles down the road, he knew farming very well even though he was in his 20s like Ron.

"Ted, how is it that you are able to take all this time away from your parent's farm in order to help us out here?"

"My folks really don't have much of a farm anymore. It has never been very large; just big enough for them to make a modest living. Your offer to pay me for taking care of your place goes a long way in helping to support my folks. I want to especially thank you for making that possible."

"Ted, I'm really thankful that you are available to help, especially since Ron is going through a rough time with his physical problems. He has just finished recovering from the staph infection but it will take him awhile before he is ready for a hip replacement.

"He and Nora will be home about Wednesday of next week. Would you be willing to stay on and help me with the farm until

Ron is up and able to do it again? It would probably be at least another six weeks or two months."

Ted said that he was really happy to help and grateful for the money that would continue to come in for that length of time. It would surely be a help to his folks.

"What else have you been thinking about having Ted do?"

"What do you mean?" I asked in a half whisper.

"Well, weren't you thinking about who to get to open up and run the Feed and Seed Store? All your neighbor farmers are going to need seed for planting and feed for their animals. Don't you think Ted is qualified?"

"Yeah! So, Ted, how would you like a permanent job once Ron is up and able to help me on the farm?"

"What kind of a job, Mr. Edwards?"

"Well, I was thinking that we need to get the Feed and Seed store up and running again. You know all the farmers. You understand what they need in the way of seed and feed, so how would you like to take on the job of managing the store for us? I don't know how to do it because my folks bought the store after I ran a -uh, left home, and I haven't worked on a farm in years."

"Wow, Mr. Edwards," he said, "after knowing all that happened at the store that caused it to be closed down, do you think I'm the one that has enough experience and know-how to make it work? I don't want to mess up."

"I think you are exactly the one, Ted. You have proven yourself to be a trustworthy man while we have been gone these couple of months. The farm is in excellent shape and the animals are all healthy and well cared for. You know what you are doing. I would trust you implicitly with the store. Besides that, Ron feels exactly like I do about you taking it over. We have talked about it quite a bit as we were figuring out what to do with it."

"Thank you for your confidence, Mr. Edwards. I really would like to work for you. I would also have been happy to work for my dad on our place, but the farm is really not big enough for two of us to work it nor is it able to bring in enough income to support us. I'm just glad I can earn some money to help meet expenses."

"I'm sorry to hear that the farm is not producing Ted. I'm sure your dad is doing the best he can to make the place productive, but I understand that right now the farm economy is apparently not as good as it was. .Let's hope that it gets turned around before long.

"Ted," I continued, "I'm glad we are able to help provide some income for your folks and from what I've seen of your work, you're as qualified as anyone I know to do what we need to have done. When Ron gets here we'll talk about it together, Okay?"

"That's Okay with me, Mr. Edwards. I need the work."

During the next few days Ted and I took opportunity to go into town and do some clean up and repair work at the Feed and Seed Store. It needed a lot of work to get it ready for opening but we had plenty of time since Ron would need to heal up and able to work on the farm before Ted would be free to get the store fully functional.

There are times, like now, when I have such a full feeling inside I just want to stand, stare at the sky, shake my head in wonder - and smile. "*I ran away from this?*"

CHAPTER 32

The day broke with sun shining, birds singing, roosters crowing, hens clucking, cows mooing and my heart pounding. I couldn't tell which was the loudest. It was Wednesday, the day on which Nora and Ron would be arriving in Pryor. They had called when they left Portland and again last night to let Ted and me know they were well on their way and would arrive here sometime in the afternoon.

That gave me time to clean up the house. It wouldn't look the same as when mom and grandma used to whip it into shape and make it shine, but at least the dishes would be out of the sink and in the cupboards where they belonged.

Ted and I did the morning chores and when those were finished I conscripted him to do some of the housework. He had kept it in pretty good shape all the while Ron and I were in Portland so I figured he could help me clean it up.

After all, I helped him in the barn. Seemed like turn-about's fair play. I heard that somewhere and I wasn't quite sure what it meant, but I thought it might be a good argument if he offered any resistance. He didn't, so we had the place straightened up in short order.

Time began to drag. One o'clock turned into two and then into three. I began to be a little anxious wondering if they had had a flat tire or an accident or ran out of gas or a half dozen other things that niggle in a person's mind when things don't go exactly as planned.

Finally, I saw the car turn off the highway and onto the lane that leads up to the house. I sprang out of the front porch swing in which I had been setting and watching for the past two hours and headed down the walk to greet them.

I tried not to look too eager. So, when the car stopped, I made an effort at casually strolling over to Nora's side of the car, opening the door and helping her get out. Once she was standing up all sense of casualness left. I put my arms around her, gave her a solid squeeze and planted a long and arduous kiss, smack on her lips.

"Lee Edwards," she said out of the side of her mouth that wasn't pressed against mine, "what in the world are you doing?"

"I'm kissing you," I said out of the side of my mouth that wasn't pressed against hers.

We both broke into uncontrollable laughter as we continued to hug each other. I looked over her shoulder to see Ron still sitting in the car, looking at us, and just shaking his head back and forth with a big grin on his face.

"What are you grinning at?" I asked him. "Haven't you ever seen two grown people kissing and hugging each other before?"

He just kept grinning and shaking his head.

Ted walked up to Ron's side of the car, opened the door and helped him get out. They were really happy to see each other for they had become the best of friends through school and occasionally helping each other out on the respective farms. They were actually more like brothers.

It was good to see the smiles exchanged between them and the usual hugs and pounding of each other on the backs. Male bonding! I noticed that Ted was very careful not to pound too hard, not knowing exactly how well Ron was doing following his surgery and long rehabilitation sessions.

As I looked at Ron I noticed that he really looked better than I had seen him in a long time. He still walked with his cane, but he had good color and a cheerful outlook. Nora had obviously taken superlative care of him.

Nora and I walked to the side of the car where Ted and Ron were standing. I embraced Ron and told him how happy I was to see him and so glad to have him home.

He said, without the slightest hesitation, "Dad, if you don't marry her, I'm going to!"

"Ron!" I blurted out. "What kind of a remark is that? Who has said anything about marriage? Nora and I have hardly had time to get to know each other and I may not be the one she wants to spend the rest of her life with and...." I didn't know what else to say.

"Well," Ron said, "you're all she's talked about for the last week. Lee this, Lee that, Lee, Lee, Lee. Dad, marry her so that she will quit talking about you and I won't have to listen to it anymore."

Ted spoke up and said, "I made some iced tea if anyone wants to come on in the house and get some."

Ron said, "I think that's a great idea, Ted. Let's go have some tea and leave these two to get to know each other."

Nora and I followed Ron and Ted as they turned to go into the house. We walked up onto the front porch and sat down on the swing and just sat there with our personal thoughts for awhile. Then we both looked at each other and began to speak at the same time.

"Nora/Lee." Both of us were silent, then "Lee/Nora." We burst out into laughing, partly because we really didn't know how to respond to Ron's impulsive statement out by the car, but also partly because we were eager to say something to express our true feeling to each other.

Finally Nora said, "You go first."

"Okay, me first," I said. "I'm glad I get to go first because I have been thinking for a week about what I would say to you when you arrived. When you told me on the phone that you loved me, I could hardly believe my ears and I simply said that I loved you too. Then before I even put the receiver down it suddenly dawned on me what you had said and how I so casually responded to it.

"It hit me like a Mac Truck, 'She said she loves me and, what's more, I know that I love her.' So I phoned you right back to tell you so. Ever since then that is just about all I can think about, how much I have come to love you and how very special you are. I do want to get to know you better and better and have you get to know me.

"Nora, I want you to hear what I have to say because I think it is important if you and I are to have any thought of a future with each other."

"What is it, Lee?" What do you feel you need to tell me?"

"Well," I said, "It is obvious, with Ron as my twenty five year old son, that somewhere along the way I made some wrong choices when I was a teenager. I was sorry that it happened then and tried to run away from it and pretend it never happened. It didn't work. Oh, it worked for awhile because I chose to forget about it, but it wouldn't stay forgotten.

"Then I had a dream. Actually it was more like a nightmare. A nightmare that compelled me to return back here to Pryor, the place of my birth. I knew I had to face the thing that had been haunting me through the intervening years of my life. I am now forty three years old, a failure in all my relationships with women – what few with whom I have related, and here I am.

"When I was a kid I thought I loved Ron's mom, Bonnie, but later discovered that it was partly love, but mostly lust. Nevertheless, once I came back to Pryor and met Ron, I simply could not feel sorry for what happened between his mom and me. He is too special to not be celebrated for who he is. I love him and would give my life for him. I really mean that. It's not just a cliche.

"However, I struggled with that same lust issue for much of my adult life, that is, until I met you. It is no longer there. Not that you aren't desirable, for you are, but I realized I respected you too much to insist on anything but a desire to be good friends.

"When I saw the way you worked with my mom and the other people in the nursing home I found myself looking at a woman who has great integrity and with the ability to care for and love people in a way that I envied. You worked tirelessly to make sure their needs were met, even when you were worn out yourself.

"I think my love for you really took root when you offered to help with Ron and then you came all the way to Portland to be there with him and said that you would stay as long as you were needed. I realized then that I really wanted you around forever.

"Nora, I love you. Like I told Ron, you may not want me, but I know in my heart that I want to spend the rest of my life with you. Will you marry me?"

We just looked at each other for a long moment.

"The real question is, Lee, do you want to marry me? You have never once asked about my past, where I came from, about my family or anything that would let you really know me. You have known me for only these few short months, but mostly at a distance.

"Nora," I said, "I think the person I have come to know in these few months is the very person with whom I want to share the rest of my life. I ask you again, "Will you marry me?"

She continued, "Lee, I think before your question can be answered, you need to hear something of who I am and what has happened to make me the person that I am today. You may not want to spend the rest of your life with me.

"I was born in Dallas to a fairly well-to-do couple, both professional people, Ray and Marie Miller. My mother is a professor in college and my dad is presently working in the oil industry, as an engineer, drilling offshore wells. He has been doing that since he was a young man and both of them are happy with what they are doing. They are there for each other. They role-modeled the kind of marriage I always dreamed of having for myself.

"I have one sister and one brother, both of whom have finished graduate work and are presently teaching in public schools. We are a very close-knit family and keep in touch on a regular basis. In fact, I called my parents last night to let them know that we had left Portland and were almost in Pryor.

"I have been married once. I married a college sweetheart, believing that our principles and moral standards were compatible. He was studying to be a medical lab technician and put in a lot of effort to make sure he passed all the tests. I helped him through because I thought it would be great that we were both interested in the medical field. I enjoyed helping him and having him help me.

"We agreed that we would remain celibate and save ourselves for each other. Because of that I thought we shared the same faith and desired the same goals for our lives.

"We had known each other for at least a year and talked many times about how important it is to be totally committed to the one with whom we planned to spend the rest of our lives as husband and wife.

"We both knew that being in our particular profession there would probably be times when the demands of our work would interfere with personal times that we would like to have together. We both agreed that it could be worked out as long as we worked at it.

"Shortly after we were married it seemed that his work demanded more and more of his time. My own schedules were flexible. Sometimes our two schedules worked for our benefit, sometimes they did not. Probably because of that I failed to take notice that we had less and less time together. Even when we did have time he would often receive a call to come to work. He would excuse himself and then be gone, sometimes for the rest of the night.

"Soon it became evident that he was not really at work nor did his lab call for his help. One night another lab technician that I happened to know called and asked if he was home. I said no, he had been called in to work at the lab that night. Wasn't he there? No, they said, he is not here and hasn't been here.

"Well, it turned out that he had been seeing another woman and using the lab as an excuse for being gone. In fact, he had been seeing other women while we were engaged and after the two of us had agreed that we would remain celibate until our marriage. That marriage lasted less than one year.

"It was a messy divorce. I truly don't know why I ever married him in the first place. I kept telling myself that I should have been able to see what he was like.

"I have been single for the past fifteen years. It has been very difficult for me to relate to another man because I was burned once and I vowed to myself that it would never happen again.

"I have gone through some counseling following the divorce and the counselor has helped me work through some of my negative attitudes regarding betrayal of vows that were taken when we got married. I meant those vows when I repeated them. He didn't. The counselor reminded me that my "truster" had been broken, it needed to be healed and I needed to learn to trust again.

"Little by little I have learned to have more trust of men. Though I will have to say that I have met a few since my divorce that have only served to remind me that most men have only one thing in mind when they go out with a woman. That wasn't for me and I told them so. I emphasized what I told one guy by slapping his filthy mouth.

"Dating has not been a part of my life for the past five years. I'm forty two years old and you're the first man around with whom I have felt safe – apart from Ron. I watched Ron with your mom at the nursing home and began to see that there really are decent men left in the world. I was old enough to be his mother, but he showed by the way he lived and acted that he was genuine and so he helped to restore my faith in men. I'm sure he's not even aware of it and he doesn't need to know it.

"When I saw the two of you at the nursing home and learned that he was your son, I had my suspicions about you. You looked awfully young to have a son that age. Once again the guard came up inside me and I was tempted to place you in the same category as those men whose only goal was to make a conquest of a woman.

"However, the more I was around you and got to know you, I found that many of the qualities that were in Ron's life also showed up in yours. It didn't take long to see that you were real and however it happened that Ron came to be your son, there was probably a somewhat logical explanation. At least that is what I began to tell myself. After awhile I began to trust all over again.

"Lee, no one was any more surprised than me when I told you over the phone that I loved you. After we hung up I had to quiz myself whether I had actually said something like that, only to have you call back immediately to remind me of what I had said and to tell me that you loved me.

"I do think that if marriage is in our future we need to have plenty of time to work through these and other issues in our lives so that we don't drag into that marriage all the baggage from the past. Don't you agree?"

"Oh, by all means, I agree," I said. "Let's take all the time we need to get to know each other, work through the issues, find out what is going to happen with Ron's hip replacement, how to get the Feed and Seed Store up and running again, get my stuff from Portland to here and the multitude of other things that needs to be done. I think it's a great idea to give ourselves plenty of time. Could we get married next week?"

"Lee Edwards, did you hear anything that I told you?"

"Nora, I have heard every word that you said to me and it makes me love you all the more. I know there is lots more to learn about you and lots for you to learn about me, but we have the rest of our lives to discover what that is.

"I have also tried to let you know about myself and the things that made me who I am. To my knowledge, I have hidden nothing from you, except what we can learn together in the future. I hope that what I have told you will make you love me all the more.

"Nora, we are not kids. We are both in our forties and we have lived half our lives. We have both had difficult and painful experiences. We have each, in our own way, tried to run away from those hard times and attempted to isolate ourselves from any more hurt. In the process we have both learned, I think, that we can't deny our past or run away from it. So I guess we have to acknowledge that there have been some failures, and maybe we can learn something from them, but they don't have to determine the rest of our lives for us, do they?

"Nora, if and when the time comes that you desire to be married, I want you to desire to be married to me. Okay?"

"I will most certainly give that some very serious thought, Lee. You are right. There a lot of things to do before we make such an important decision. We need to think about Ron's continued therapy, what you are going to do with the farm and feed store and all the other things you mentioned awhile ago. While you two are doing all that, I need to get back to my job and make sure that I still have a job at Mary-Martha.

"Lee, what would you think about doing it after Ron's hip replacement so that he can be your best man?"

"Sounds like a workable plan to me. Wonder if we could get the doctors to agree to a hip replacement next week?"

"Lee Edwards!"

CHAPTER 33

Neighbors had come in to help Ted harvest what corn crop had been planted, summer had come and gone, schools were back in session, things were quieting down in Pryor and Ron had spent the summer gaining new strength. He even ventured to ride on one of the "corn-pickers," harvesting the corn. He seemed to be right in the height of his glory. He loved planting and harvesting the corn crops. He said he liked the smell of the silk and the tassel, especially after a hot summer day. Frankly, I think he was influenced by his grandpa. He was also a romantic.

Fall was in the air.

Arrangements were made for Ron to be admitted to the Roberts Medical Center in Memphis. By this time he was totally healed from the serious infections that he had suffered several months earlier. He had become strong in his body and after a trip to Memphis and consultation with the medical staff at the Center it was determined that he was an excellent candidate for the hip surgery.

Following the necessary consultations and preparations, Ron had a total hip replacement. The surgery went better than the doctors had expected. After a few days of Ron being in recovery at the hospital, Nora convinced the medical team that Pryor had an excellent rehabilitation and care facility where Ron would receive the best of care. They agreed, on her say so, that they would release Ron to that excellent rehabilitation and care facility in Pryor.

What Nora failed to tell them was that it was a nursing home where she worked and that she would be the sole rehabilitator.

Ron was transported back to Pryor and entered the Mary-Martha Nursing Home - rehab section, where he received first class treatment by everyone on the staff who remembered him from the many times he had been there with my mom. Personally I think he really enjoyed the personal attention he received from all the young nurses' aides as well as from Nora.

I also noticed that Ted visited him regularly and each time he did there were two nurses aides that always seemed to appear in Ron's room to take care of whatever needs he might conjure up with which he needed help. The four of them became quite an item of "information sharing" among the rest of the staff at the Mary Martha "rehabilitation and care center."

Nora kept me informed about what she thought were some serious relationships that were developing between the two young aides and Ron and Ted. Frankly, I think his healing took longer than needed.

Ultimately his hip was completely healed within about six weeks. With regular physical therapy he learned to walk without even a hint of a limp. There was always a young volunteer to help Nora with the PT.

The day of his release was truly a day to celebrate. It had been almost six years since his hip was crushed in the accident and he had spent much of that time confined either to a hospital bed or limping on a leg that painfully curtailed any activity other than taking care of basic necessities.

"Now," he shouted, "I am not only pain-free, I am cane-free!"

It was getting close to Christmas, so we had a big party at the farm to celebrate Ron's homecoming. Snow had begun to fall, but not enough to hamper driving conditions or dampen a party spirit.

People came from the excellent care and rehabilitation center, aka Mary-Martha Nursing Home, from neighboring farms and from all over Pryor. Almost everyone had a share in Ron's painful losses and years of being crippled. Now they wanted to share in the joyous occasion of him being pain-free, cane-free and able to enjoy his young life again.

Many brought presents. It was Christmas time and they felt it was a great time to give gifts. I had to remind them that they were spoiling my kid and he would be expecting more of the same once they departed and, what's more, he will expect it even after he is fully recovered. That didn't impress anyone. He was treated as though he was everyone's grandson.

The next day I drove into Pryor to pick up some supplies at Ben's convenience store. When I entered, Ben asked, "Lee, have you seen today's County Free Press?"

"No, Ben. What's in it beside the local gossip column?"

"You'll be interested to see the headlines. Here, take a look."

He handed me the local County newspaper, a weekly edition that really did do quite a good job in reporting the news in an objective way, as well as providing information for the farmers regarding prices, weather reports and other information that could be used to benefit them.

The part I always liked about the paper, even as a kid, was the reporting of what happened in the town a year ago, two years ago, ten years ago and so forth. It was like reading a part of the town's history each week.

The headline read "FORMER SHERIFF CONVICTED," followed by the details. *"Former County Sheriff, Jerry Burdett, has been formally charged and convicted of complicity in the embezzlement of several thousands of dollars from the Edwards' Feed and Seed Store located in Pryor.*

"The crime was perpetrated by his nephew, Clint Burdett, who implicated the former Sheriff during the court hearing and who is now serving time in the state pen.

The newspaper article continued, *"Jerry Burdett has also been convicted of a cover-up related to an accident six years ago that killed Mr. C. J. Edwards, a long time resident and community leader of Pryor. Clint Burdett was convicted of vehicular homicide in that accident. Former Sheriff Burdett knew how it happened, but failed to investigate the accident or reveal his knowledge of the one who was responsible. He, along with his nephew, has been sentenced to serve time in prison for both crimes.*

"A spokesperson for The Insurance Company that brought the charges states that they feel that justice has been served." End quote.

"Wow, Ben," I said, "I wasn't even aware what had been happening relative to that case. I have been so involved in Ron's illness, his rehabilitation and also the hip replacement that I totally forgot about the court hearing we had."

"That's no problem, Lee. You told me to represent the Edwards' family interest. I have been doing that and didn't feel any need to inform you as to what was happening until some kind of verdict was reached.

"The embezzlement charges were pretty much wrapped up at the original court hearing and the thing with Sheriff Burdett was handled by my friend Fred and me. Remember, he's my lawyer friend from Fayetteville that had Clint arrested? We have been working together and personally, I think we did a rather good job."

"You sure did, Ben. Remind me to get a check in the mail to you as soon as possible."

"Okay," he said. "consider yourself reminded."

CHAPTER 34

"Thank you, Reverend Reinfeld," Nora said. "We will be there at 2:00 o'clock on Friday afternoon for the counseling session." Then she turned and said to me. "There, it's all set. He will see us on Friday at 2:00."

Nora and I had finally made the decision that we wanted to be married to each other for the rest of our lives. I don't remember if it was I who asked her first or she who asked me. At any rate, I said "yes" when she asked me.

We had taken the time to get to know each other as she continued to work at the Mary-Martha Nursing Home and I pitched in at the farm to help with fixing and repairing what needed to be fixed and repaired.

We also took opportunity to have lunch and dinner together on a regular basis. Those were always special times of sharing tidbits about ourselves and me asking questions like "Where shall we go on our honeymoon?"

"How do you like my hair, Lee? I went to the beauty parlor yesterday. Did you even notice?"

I noticed that I have yet a lot to learn. Make a note to yourself, Lee, for future reference: *"Don't forget to mention her hair, Lee."*

Ron and I painted what needed to be painted, and oiled the machinery that needed to be oiled in order to get it ready for spring plowing. Days were beginning to warm up and the ground began to dry out. In a few weeks it would be ready for plowing and planting of corn once again.

When I suggested that we might try wheat this year it was suggested that I might like to sleep in the barn. Dad had totally brainwashed Ron as to the superior crop in this part of the country.

Friday came and I picked Nora up at her place and we went to Reverend Reinfeld's office at the church for the agreed upon counseling session. I wasn't all that convinced that we needed counseling. After all, we were both in our forties and surely he could tell us very little more than we already know about being married.

"Good afternoon Nora and Lee, welcome," the Reverend said when he greeted us. "Come in, please. Be seated and make yourselves comfortable."

It was a comfortable setting and he made us feel very much at ease. I think he could see that I wasn't quite sure that I needed this kind of thing. My attitude about churchy things had not improved much since my return from my venture out into the world beyond Pryor.

After some general chit chat as to how we are and how he is, he got right down to business. "Now tell me," he said, "why do you want to get married?"

Nora and I looked at each other, hoping the other person would answer the question first. Her look appeared to indicate that I was to go first.

"Well, Reverend," I said, while scratching the back of my head and trying to think of how to begin, "I want to get married to Nora…. well, because I love her." That should do it, I thought!

"That's a great start," he said. "Now what do you mean by the statement that you love her."

"*Gosh*," I thought, "*doesn't everyone know what it means when a person says 'I love you?'*"

"Well," I said, still scratching and trying to think again, "When I tell Nora I love her I am telling her that she is that special person in my life. I want to be there for her, take care of her, share her life with her and that kind of stuff."

"Okay. Thank you Lee. That's a pretty good start."

I was pleased.

"Nora, why do you want to marry this man who says that you are special and he wants to be there for you, take care of you and share your life with you and that kind of stuff?"

"Well, Reverend Steinfeld, Lee and I have known each other for almost a year now. I think in that period of time we have learned a lot not only about the other person, but also about ourselves. We have shared a lot about our weaknesses, our strengths and our desire to have our lives count for something. We have also talked about what we will be bringing into the marriage that the other person should know about so that there are no surprises."

I thought, "*Why didn't I think of saying something like that? Why do women always seem to have the better answer?*"

"And besides," she added with a glint in her eyes as she looked at me, "almost every day we have lunch and dinner together at either his place or mine. We have decided that we would also like to have breakfast together at his place."

In that simple statement the Reverend must have caught on to the fact that though we had developed a close and loving relationship we had both made a decision to refrain from sexual intimacy until we are married. We knew it went against much of what is touted in the promiscuous culture in which we lived, but, based on our past, it was what we wanted and we stuck with it.

"Breakfast is a great meal to have together," he said.

After some other basic talking about the importance of communication, shared faith, commitment and so on, the session ended with the Reverend saying, "Our next counseling session will include a discussion of the vows that you will be taking during the wedding ceremony. Those vows are very important so I have written out a copy for you to take with you and think about before we get together again. Would next Friday at 2:00 o'clock be a good time for you?"

I was thinking, *"Wow, I made it through one session and now he wants us back for another one?"*

"Yes," Nora agreed "that will be fine."

"Sure, oh sure," I said. "That will be perfectly fine with me."

"Oh, and yes," he said. "I almost forgot a very important thing. I want you to go home today and write a letter to each other over the weekend, mail it on Monday, even though you live here in the same town, and bring it with you to next Friday's session. We will talk about it then.

"A letter? What do you want us to put in it?" I asked.

"Your letter will answer the question I asked you at the beginning of today's session: "Why do you want to get married in the first place? You will write in your letter, "This is why I want to marry you. These are the strengths I will be bringing into our marriage. These are my known weaknesses that we will be dealing with. This is what I have to give to our marriage. These are some of my hopes for our future together. I think that will give you a little more time to think about it than I gave you to answer it today."

"Reverend," I asked. "Why is it necessary to do this? Didn't we already answer the question for you?"

"Yes, as a matter of fact, you did," he said. However, you told it to me, not to each other. And the reason I am having you do this is because just recently I had a counseling session with a couple who are having major trouble in their marriage that may well end up in a divorce unless something miraculous happens. I heard one of them say to the other one, 'I don't know why I ever married you in the first place.' I want couples to know why they are getting married in the first place."

We left his office with that statement ringing in our ears. We took his advice and committed ourselves to writing the letters. It was an especially poignant statement for Nora. I'm sure she remembered that she had told me that she did not know why she had married her husband in the first place.

It also made me give serious thought about what I had done to Ron's mother in the first place.

.

CHAPTER 35

During the weekend I checked in at the Edwards' Feed and Seed Store of Pryor to see how Ted was doing with the business. That's what we named it, the

Edwards' Feed and Seed Store of Pryor,

Ted Russell, General Manager,

We decided to name it that in order to honor the two people that had done so much to help the people of Pryor through the hard times, and also as a reminder to the community that it was locally owned.

Following harvest we put all our efforts into getting the store up and running again.

The severance check I received when I was fired from the Law firm in Portland had arrived. That, plus some of the funds from the sale of the condo, provided ample money for whatever was needed to re-open the store after being closed for so long.

I had also checked with the financial advisor that I had in Portland to see how my investments were doing. He informed me that the returns had been very good. I asked him to send me a check, which he did, and I banked both the capital gains checks from the condo and the investments in a local bank – First Prairie Bank of Pryor. I could have used one of the other banks, but I chose this one.

I felt good making that deposit, hoping that Mr. Hooper, the president of the First Prairie Bank of Pryor, would see the amount of the deposit and be impressed. He was one of the ones who kept saying to me, "Lee, why don't you make something of yourself." I wanted him to see that I did.

Ted wanted to make the Edwards' Feed and Seed Store of Pryor a profitable business for the community and, I think, to show the community how much it needed the store. I also think that he wanted to show all of us that he, a local man like Clint Burdett, could make it productive through honesty and hard work without siphoning off the proceeds for himself.

He was very careful to have the books audited on a regular basis and then set down with me to go over the records. Finally I told him that I didn't need to be in on everything because I trusted him and Ben who had audited the books all along. He seemed pleased that I would trust him with the business and, as a result, it appeared that he worked even harder.

When spring came and it was time to plow and plant the fields again, local farmers returned to purchase their supplies at the Edwards' Feed and Seed Store of Pryor. Ted was able to fill their orders at good prices while still making a profit. The store prospered and Ted was a very proud young man. So was Ron. So was I.

Ron and I continued to work at the farm and I began to relearn the things that I had forgotten how to do. Even though I had been gone for some twenty five years, the things I learned as a kid on the farm came back to me little by little.

Ron was also a great help. He had his own little ways of showing me how to do something without giving me the idea that I did not know what I was doing, which, most of the time I didn't. I had learned some from Ted, but I think he was timid about telling me I didn't know what I was doing.

How do you milk a cow? We didn't have enough of a herd anymore to warrant having automatic milking machines. While I was trying to learn how to milk again, the poor old cows would look back at me with those huge eyes, wide with wonder and amazement. I think they were trying to say, "Why don't you go and get Ron or Ted? They know how to do it." Or "Your hands are cold. Warm 'em up or get 'em off my body or I'll kill you." Even the cows had been influenced by my mom. Their moooos sounded more like grrrrrrrs.

How do you saddle a horse and make the cinch strap tight enough so that when you put your foot in the stirrup in an attempt to mount, you and the saddle don't wind up under the horse's belly?

Little by little, week by week and finally month by month I began to get the hang of farming again, the thing I vowed I never wanted to do. It really didn't feel bad doing it. However, hands that were used to filing cabinets, briefcases, computers and post-it note pads, had to get used to blisters, calluses and splinters under the finger nails - what fingernails were left.

I will obviously have to figure out some way to wear gloves at my wedding.

Nora and I had our four counseling sessions with the Reverend. I thought there was going to be only one, but as it turned out I probably needed six. He required only four. There was a lot to learn about being married. Since I had never been married I did need to learn a lot. Since Nora's marriage had ended on the rocks, she needed to unlearn a lot.

The letters we wrote to each other were really helpful in letting us get to know more about ourselves, about each other and how much we really did want to be married. I knew I would never say "I really don't know why I married you in the first place," because now we both knew why. We really did love each other and for all the right reasons.

As Nora and I discussed the letters we decided that in those times when we had major disagreements or arguments or lost our ability to communicate we would drag them out and re-read them as a reminder of our commitment to each other.

When the last counseling session was finished the Reverend told us that he would be honored to perform the ceremony. He felt that we were both mature enough to make the marriage work. That was kind of him since we're both in our forties, I should hope so.

He did say that he was making some concessions because he generally refused to marry persons who had been divorced and persons with children born out of wedlock.

Since Nora's marriage ended because of adultery committed by her husband and because I was young and *ignorant* – he seemed to have put extra emphasis on that word, at the time when Ron was conceived, he would be willing to help both of us start a new life together.

The wedding day had been set for several months. It would be on a Saturday at 2:00 in the afternoon. We tried to put it at a time when the early spring field work would be done and all the neighbors and friends in and around Pryor would be able to attend. It turned out to be perfect timing with perfect weather for the occasion.

Invitations were sent out to practically everyone in the county and when the day came everyone gathered at the Trinity Community Church of Pryor where the Reverend Robert Reinfeld would conduct the marriage ceremony for Mr. Lee Edwards and Miss Nora Miller

I think the ceremony came off without a hitch. I can't say for sure as I spent my time looking at Nora. I think I remember repeating the vows that the Reverend had talked with us about and

I also think that I remember putting a ring on her finger and her placing one on mine. My mind seemed to be focused elsewhere.

I did hear him say, "I now pronounce you husband and wife together. Those that God joins together, don't let man mess it up." Or something like that. At least that's the way I interpreted it. I don't think I ever did understand the word "asunder" even as we went through it at rehearsal.

Then the part of the ceremony that I really liked, "The groom may kiss the bride." That came through loud and clear.

When I looked into her beautiful eyes and saw that captivating smile I lost track of everything else that happened in the ceremony. All I could think was, can we skip the reception? In fact when I kissed her I said, out of the side of my mouth, "Honey, let's skip the reception and get on with the honeymoon."

"Lee," she said out the side of her mouth, "we will do no such thing. These people have come for the wedding and reception and we will remain here until it's over."

I learned right off that she knows how to give orders.

Ron and Ted had stood with me as my Best Man and Groomsman, respectively. We had contacted Nora's family to see if they would want to be a part of the wedding, but they could not attend. Mother had classes to teach and exams to administer. Dad was out drilling in the ocean somewhere. Likewise with her siblings, they were involved with teaching and, try as they would, they could not get away.

I felt sorry for Nora because it would have meant a lot to have them there. However, she did have two of her nurse friends – or, were they Ron and Ted's nurse friends, from Mary-Martha stand with her as her Maid of Honor and Bridesmaid. One was Susan and I think the other girl was Cindy. They had become like family to Nora and apparently getting fairly close to being that with Ron and Ted. I noticed they looked at each other a lot during the ceremony.

Following the Guinness World Book of Records wedding kiss, the Reverend cleared his throat and said, "Ladies and Gentlemen, may I introduce Mr. & Mrs. Lee Edwards. Everyone broke into thunderous applause, Mrs. Orrin Webb began to play some lively music on the organ and we headed down the aisle to exit the sanctuary.

"Let's just keep going, get in the car and head out of town," I pleaded and begged with Nora. "That will be far more fun than standing in a reception line and having you jam a piece of cake in my mouth and cameras flashing all over the place. Huh? Can we?"

"Lee, you make it very tempting, but the answer is still no. We need to greet our wedding guests," she insisted. "And besides that, we need to sign the marriage certificate. Remember? The Reverend told us that we would do it at the reception."

"I'll just bet that he did that in order to make sure we stayed for the reception," I whined.

We had already had our first disagreement and we hadn't even gotten out of the center aisle of the church. I probably should re-read the letter I wrote before we go on our honeymoon.

I did notice that we didn't stay very long at the reception before Nora suggested that we might want to cut it short and get on the road before it gets dark.

"Yes!" I said, as I pumped my right arm with the thumb up in the air. It was only 3:30 in the afternoon and the sun had hours before it went down. We do need to leave before it gets dark.

Finally the reception ended and people began making their way out of the building. Nora and I managed to stay through the whole thing and even shake hands and receive the well-wishes of those who attended. It seemed like we shook hands with everyone in the whole county. My face hurt from smiling all day long.

CHAPTER 36

At last! We climbed into our car, with the top down, and headed for that private place where we had arranged for a two week honeymoon. It was a secret place no one was to know about and those who did know about it were sworn to secrecy or else it could kill them – they being Ron and Ted. I had also learned something from my mother.

When couples plan their honeymoon, some like to go on cruises, others like to go to a far off island, others like to hike mountain trails, others like to go to the seaside and still others like to stay home. Nora and I were in the last group.

We had our honeymoon place all picked out and we planned ahead on how to handle it. We rented a twenty four foot trailer and put it out beside one of three groves of trees, now full grown. We had total privacy because only two people we loved and trusted knew where we were and the trailer could not be seen from the main house.

They knew that if they broke that trust and revealed our secret rendezvous or hideout, they would suffer the fate that mom often promised to the wayward - "it could kill you."   The lake was a perfect place for peace and quiet and to begin our life as husband and wife.

We stocked the cupboards with the kinds of food we liked, rolled out the awning on the trailer, put chairs and tables outside, with a couple of chaise lounges by the water's edge and settled in for a two week retreat from the rest of the world.

We spent our time eating, swimming, sun-bathing, sleeping while wrapped in each other's arms and generally acting like newlyweds. What are the words of the song, "Getting to know you, getting to know all about you?" Well, maybe not all about each other, because we had only two weeks, but we figured we had the rest of our lives to find out about all the other things we didn't learn about by the lake.

Amazingly, the farm as well as Edwards' Feed and Seed Store of Pryor both survived without my incompetent oversight. Also amazingly, Mary-Martha Nursing Home was able to continue its excellent rating of service without Nora's competent presence. We were both somewhat perplexed that people could do quite well without us being there to direct the activities.

However, both Ron and Ted were very pleased to have us at the farm house. While Nora and I were spending time "getting to know each other out by the lake," as they put it, they moved Nora's household articles from her place out to the farm by using one of the seed trucks to haul the furniture. It was large enough to haul just about everything in one load. It was all there when our honeymoon was over. There was plenty of room in the big house to place what could be used and also store what we would not be using on a regular basis. The attic was great for storing other things.

The honeymoon at the lake came to an end. However, the lifelong honeymoon was just beginning and I was hoping that it would never end.

CHAPTER 37

Nora and I loved to sit on the swing following a busy day's work and enjoy the twilight time in quiet conversations.

One evening we sat on the front porch swing just as the evening sun was setting in the west, casting a beautiful golden glow over the fields and painting the very tops of the trees with light that reflected into the developing shadows around the house. What a special time of day!

"Lee," Nora whispered, as she squeezed my hand and laid her head over on my shoulder, "I am so happy. This is such a special place. I am glad that we get to spend the rest of our lives here together."

"I'm happy too," I replied. "However, we'll have to ask Ron if we can stay here the rest of our lives because it all belongs to him. My dad made that provision for him in his will."

Then I told her about the circumstances that brought about the change in the will. I had failed to tell her that little detail during all our times of getting to know each other and finding out everything that needed to be found out. I was now concerned about how she would respond with that bit of new information.

"Lee," she said, as she kept her head on my shoulder. "Do you think he would let us rent a spot down by the lake and put a trailer or something on it? I don't need a big house. I could be happy any place as long as you and I are together."

"Me, too," I said, relieved that she didn't take me to task for failing to tell her about the house and farm.

We sat there with my arm around her shoulders and watched the sun set.

"Lee, have you ever thought about the sun rising and setting?"

"Well, Nora, I really haven't put a lot of thought into it. I have watched it happen on occasion. I just assumed that it would be a daily occurrence since it has been happening on a regular basis for a fairly long period of time."

"I mean, have you ever considered that there was a time when everyone thought the earth was flat and stationary and the sun revolved around it? Then it was discovered that the earth was not flat and it was the sun that was the center of our galaxy and we rotated around it."

"Yes, Nora, I do remember learning something about that bit of scientific wisdom in a science class way back in high school. So what's your point?"

With her head still on my shoulder and gazing now at the diminishing grey and white streaks of light just above the horizon, she continued, "Well, we live in a very scientific age, right?

"Right!"

"And we can calculate by way of the weather satellites the movement of clouds, the high and low pressures that tell us if it's going to be stormy or sunny, the wind velocity on a given day at a given time and all the other technological data available to us in this scientific age. Right?"

"Right! And...." I said, while motioning with my hand for her to continue.

"Lee, have you ever wondered why, that at the end of the weather reports each day on the radio or television, the well-trained scientist meteorologist always concludes by saying, 'sunrise will be at 6:23 a.m. and sunset at 7:41 p.m.' when it neither rises nor sets?"

"Wow! I guess I had never put much thought into that. Do you think it will have a destabilizing impact on our marriage?"

"Lee Edwards, you really need to think about such important things," she said, as she slapped my belly and arose to go into the house.

Opening the screen door, she looked back at me and, with an impish grin, said, "You really do need to keep up with important scientific information or else your brain may become destabilized."

I just looked at her and grinned.

"See what happens when you follow your heart?"

I thought, *"It has been an incredible time in my life over this past year."*

I got up from the swing, walked over to the porch rail, sat on it, leaned up against one of the pillars and gave thought about all the things that had happened since I had that nightmare about returning to Pryor, the place where I was born and from which I ran away.

I felt at home now. Like the song says, "Sometimes this old farm feels like a long lost friend. Hey it's good to be back home again."

"And what about Pryor?"

"What about Pryor?" I asked myself.

"Is it home? Does Pryor feel like home? This is the place from which you ran away. You thought it was too confining and parochial with all its community things that you wanted to forget like, the county fairs, church suppers, picnics in the park, school

plays, ball games and all the other small town stuff that goes with a place like this.

"Yeah, I thought that way, once. But since coming home to Pryor I have realized that I was a young, arrogant, scared kid who didn't appreciate all that his family and community had to offer him. I threw it away for something far less fulfilling and, in the process, missed out on a lot of things that could have been a blessing in my life."

"Do you think it was all wasted?"

"No, I don't think so. Someone or something must have been watching over me. Maybe it was mom or dad praying for me. Something happened or else I would not have had that awful nightmare that compelled me to come back here. I think I have learned that running away is not the answer to any problems I might have. I have also learned that even the stuff that seems bad at the time can somehow be turned around for my good."

"Like what?"

"Well, I've been thinking, like what Bonnie and I did. We were foolish kids, but look at who I have in my life because of it. I have a handsome and gifted son. I love Ron more than I can tell; sometimes I think I love him more than life itself.

"Even getting fired from the job I liked in Portland turned out to be a blessing. I couldn't run away anymore to Portland to get away from Pryor, so I had to stay here. But because of that I now have a close friend in Ben, and also Ted, who is like another son to me and now a business partner in the feed store. Besides that, I received enough money in the severance pay check to help with Ron's surgery and still have some for the renovation of the store.

"And too, I grieved because I got to know my mom for only a week before she died. I really wondered what good could come out of that. Then, while I was at the nursing home I met Nurse Nora, and look what I received from that, a beautiful and loving Wife Nora with whom I will be able to spend the rest of my life.

"Sometimes I think it's hard to determine that which is good and that which is bad or how it's possible to bring good stuff out of bad stuff. I wonder what my mom would have to say about that?"

CHAPTER 38

As I sat there and looked out toward Pryor, I could see that there was still enough daylight to make out the top of the town's grain elevators on the horizon. Street and store front lights had been turned on, making the town very visible in the middle of the prairie. It was dusk and the day was quickly coming to an end.

I could not help but remember the one flashing yellow light that used to be at the main intersection letting everyone know that Pryor was moving toward becoming a thriving city. It had moved closer to becoming that city, though still a small one.

I got up off the rail on which I had been setting, to follow Nora into the house. However, I had to turn around once again to see whether or not the sun had really set. It had! Or was it just the rotation of the earth? Either way, I think I'll go to bed.

"I've been hoping and praying that you would come, and you did! I'm glad you came."

I paused, as I reached for the door knob, turned and glanced back over my shoulder for just a brief second.

"Yeah! So am I."

I opened the door, walked inside and quietly closed it behind me.

ABOUT THE AUTHOR

Larry L. Eddings was born in 1933 in Broken Arrow, OK, the last of eleven children. He grew up in a migrant worker family through his high school years. The family moved to Oregon when he was ten years old. Shortly after graduation from high school he married Audrey Hamblen, his high school sweetheart. They have two children, seven grand-children and one great grandchild.

Larry, with his wife, has written multiple books and pamphlets related to their profession. One such published work is "Anointed to Heal," a book designed as curriculum for individuals or churches who desire to develop a ministry of healing and wholeness in their local group.

He has published two previous novels. In the titles of his books, he uses the names of ordinary people. In the pages of his books those people often experience out of the ordinary circumstances, only to discover they have within them extraordinary abilities to overcome.

Larry's two previous novels are "Sam" and "Invincible Shirley."

His venture into writing novels was inspired and encouraged by his son, Gary, who is a published novelist.

Made in the USA
San Bernardino, CA
03 December 2017